J.L Green

Allotments and Small Holdings

J.L Green

Allotments and Small Holdings

ISBN/EAN: 9783337397029

Printed in Europe, USA, Canada, Australia, Japan

Cover: Foto ©Andreas Hilbeck / pixelio.de

More available books at **www.hansebooks.com**

ALLOTMENTS

AND

SMALL HOLDINGS

BY

J. L. GREEN, F.S.S.,

Author of " The Rural Industries of England," "The Old Yeomen,' &c

LONDON
SWAN SONNENSCHEIN & CO. Limd.
NEW YORK: CHARLES SCRIBNER'S SONS
1896

PREFACE.

THE chief object of this little Work—apart from its general advocacy of Allotments and Small Holdings—is to show how the enactments relating thereto may be put into operation.

The technical matter, therefore—brought down to the latest date—will, it is hoped, be found useful not only to those who desire land and to land-owners, but to Parish, District, and County Councillors in whose hands the enforcement of the Allotments and Small Holdings Acts is so largely placed.

The Work — which raises no class anti-
pathies—is based upon a very extensive experience in the practical application of the
Acts in question : and to that fact mainly
will be due any merit it may be deemed to
possess.

CONTENTS.

——:0:——

		PAGE
PREFACE,	- - - - -	V.

PART I.—ALLOTMENTS.

Chap.	I. THE PEASANTRY AND THE LAND, -	-	I
„	II. LEGISLATION, - - -	-	7
„	III. HOW TO PUT THE ACTS IN MOTION,	-	25
„	IV. "ACREAGE" AND RESULTS,	-	- 30
„	V. RULES AND AGREEMENTS, -	-	- 38

PART II.—SMALL HOLDINGS.

Chap.	VI. LEGISLATION, - -	-	- 56
„	VII. THE COTTAGE AND FARM BUILDINGS DIFFICULTY, - -	-	- 70
„	VIII. COUNTY COUNCILS AND SMALL FARMS, -		94

PART III.—UNEMPLOYED AND THE LAND.

PAGE

Chap. IX. THE TOWN UNEMPLOYED AND THE LAND, -   101

APPENDICES.

ORDERS UNDER LOCAL GOVERNMENT ACT,   -   -   117

RULES UNDER SMALL HOLDINGS ACT, -   -   -   125

FURTHER RULES UNDER SMALL HOLDINGS ACT,   -   130

TYPES OF BRITISH PEASANTRY (ILLUSTRATED),   -   141

ALLOTMENTS AND SMALL HOLDINGS.

PART I.—ALLOTMENTS.

CHAPTER I.

THE PEASANTRY AND THE LAND.

THE rural cultivator below the rank of farmer belonged, up to the York and Lancaster period in the history of England, to the category of serfs, slaves, or villeins; but as that period wore on, the extinction of villeinage became an accomplished fact, and with it there gradually but surely sprang up a large and increasing number of yeomen (or small freeholders). Estates became divided in different parts throughout the country; the freeholders increased, and trade generally was augmented; with the result that there was a much greater measure of comfort amongst the whole population, and not least amongst the peasantry.

In the Tudor period which followed, it is painful to record that this progress, so far as the small farmers and

A

peasantry were concerned, received a most material check. The demand for wool was considerable, and Henry VIII. and his advisers thought this could be produced in larger quantities if the smaller farms were less numerous, and the larger farms *more* numerous. Accordingly, commerce requiring the wool, the small holdings very generally became added one to another. The merchants, too, becoming wealthy, and being desirous of land, bought out the small freeholders ; and many are the complaints of the period at the "farming gentlemen and clerking knights " [1] and others who were guilty of such a practice. Forsyth declares that the small farmers were "got rid of either by fraud or force, or tired out with repeated wrongs into parting with their property." And so on. It was largely in consequence of this state of things that Elizabeth was prompted to make her celebrated inquiry into the condition of the poor, and so to remove, if possible, the great prevailing discontent amongst the common people.

In the Stuart period, however, we find the yeomen and peasantry again in the possession or occupation of land, both classes being numerous, prosperous, and (as regards the former) influential. It was, as distinct from to-day, very common, too, for the country gentry to "spend their season " in the county towns. [2]

In the earlier part of the following period, *i.e.*, the Brunswick period, great improvement took place in the agricultural industry, owing to the action of the larger land-owners in improving their estates ; though Young sarcastically remarks that "the farming tribe is now made up of all ranks, from a duke to an apprentice." Owing, however, to the undoubtedly better cultivation of the eighteenth

---

[1] Latimer.   [2] Defoe.

century, the land yielded in corn and stock double and treble what it did in, say, the thirteenth century, whilst the sheep's fleece was four times heavier at the former date than it was at the latter.[1] Commerce also amazingly increased from the various inventions and discoveries of the time, and agriculture was again forced up to "a feverish and unhealthy prosperity." But in this same Brunswick period, right on up to within the last forty to fifty years, the small freeholders were tempted to sell (and, where only tenants, to leave) their lands, with the result that the large farm system once more became the order of the day in our agricultural economy. Common and waste lands, between 1760 and 1867, were enclosed to the extent of 7,325,439 acres, and thus the peasantry were dispossessed, or their rights bought from them, on the plea that the land which they occupied, or used, could be put to better purpose by "large farming," or *capitalist* farming. These common and waste lands were, beyond question, sometimes legally, and sometimes illegally, taken and enclosed, but always on the plea we have named, and which, let us admit, was in numerous cases a genuine plea.

The large-farm system, however, has, as every day shows, again failed. Bad seasons, want of capital, low prices, an increasing population, and the higher wages demanded by farm hands, have been the main factors conducive to this result. Some think that it would be a grand thing to be able to contemplate our labourers all fully occupied and fairly paid, and the land itself cultivated by large owners or large farmers; but it was not—is not—to be. A demand, therefore, is now made for a restitution of things more or less on the lines of former times—a demand

---

[1] Rogers.

which, in the interest of all three classes connected with the land, and in the interest of the nation as a whole, these pages, it is hoped, may assist. This "restitution" means, amongst other things, a more extended and even better cultivation; and surely it must be wise to cultivate the land to the greatest possible extent and in the best possible manner. The large-farm system is not always calculated to achieve either result. The allotment holder, who eventually becomes a small farmer, produces in many instances twice as much, *pro râta*, as does the large farmer; his produce is quite as good; and such increased production must, in the face of our growing imports, be to the advantage of the nation at large. However much we may (as we ought to) be grateful for the improvements which large land-owners and tenant farmers have brought about by the application of their capital in buying and in using machinery, draining the land, and otherwise improving it, we suppose that this does not, cannot, compensate for a divorced labouring population—a population having no real and tangible interest in life beyond the mere keeping of body and soul together by means of a weekly wage.

We can, consequently, understand the demand now made on behalf of the agricultural labouring population. That demand has for its object the retaining of such population upon the soil by means of allotments and small holdings— the keeping of it in the country, where, not contaminated with that of the towns, it may remain and thrive morally, physically, economically, and socially—being, at the same time, a firm and natural safeguard to the stability of the empire. It may be stated, and has been often stated, that large farming is more conducive to cheap production than small farming; but in reply we would say, that our experience in many parts of the country shows that large farmers do not and cannot employ sufficient labour to cultivate the land to the greatest and best extent; secondly, that the argument is, therefore, delusive; and thirdly, that the question is primarily a social one, and an economic one afterwards. This last consideration is, we fear, too often lost sight of.

To alter the unsatisfactory state of matters arising from the divorcement of the peasantry from the soil, the Legislature, by the Allotments Acts of 1887 and 1890, and subsequently by the Local Government Act, 1894, recognised, for the first time, the right of the labourers to obtain from the farmer and land-owner, by *compulsory* means, land for the purposes of cultivation—a fact of great interest.[1]   A good deal of misrepresentation as to the value of the two former Acts has been, and is even now, current.   It is asserted that the Acts were, and are, " useless."   It is a matter of experience with the writer when he declares they have been *enormously* useful.

The " demand " referred to on the previous page is entirely owing to the Right Honourable Jesse Collings, M.P., and the friends he gathered around him about the year 1880 and onwards.   In Parliament he brought forward a bill with the threefold object of securing (1) allotments, (2) small holdings, and (3) power for tenants already occupying small holdings to permanently acquire the lands in their occupation.   Mr. Collings' ceaseless work in this direction was—it is right to point out—year after year treated with indifference by members of both sides of the House; and annually, when he brought on his bill it was " counted out," " talked out," or otherwise disposed of, with but little interest being manifested in the objects it and he sought to promote. Mr. Collings, however, had seen enough of the agricultural

---

[1] See also remarks in Part II. on " Small Holdings.'

labourers to know that what he was striving for would, if adopted, prove a step—and that a most important one—in opening up a career upon the land for that class of the population which had been neglected for generations. Accordingly, after the first few years of almost single-handed effort, sufficient impression was made upon the people and their representatives in Parliament, to make it clear that before long some happy issue would accrue : in fact, the issue came with almost startling suddenness in 1887,[1] when, as we have said, the first measure containing compulsory power to take land for allotment purposes was passed into law.

---

[1] Under the Allotments Act of that year, and the Allotments Act, 1890, 5,536 persons had secured allotments, amounting in all to 2,249 acres, 2 roods, 39 poles, in England and Wales up to 28th December, 1894. These figures do not include very many thousands of persons who secured allotments direct from the landlords under the voluntary clauses of the Acts, and as to which there are no official data. A fair estimate at the same date would place the number at about 100,000 persons.

CHAPTER II.

WE propose now to give details of the legislative recog·
nition to which we have referred; and, in so doing, we
shall indicate (1) to those desiring allotments, what is, at
the present time, the procedure to be followed to acquire
them; and (2) to land-owners and local authorities the
duties which the State has placed upon them to discharge
when applied to by would-be allottees.

THE ALLOTMENTS ACT OF 1887.—The Administration
of the Act is placed in the hands of the Sanitary Authority,
which in boroughs is the Town Council, and, in rural
districts, usually the Rural District Council.   By section
2, any six Parliamentary electors, or resident ratepayers
in a district can require the Sanitary Authority to inquire
into the supply of Labourers' Allotments in their district or
parish, and it then becomes obligatory on the Local
Authority to cause an inquiry to be made.

If the Authority are satisfied that there is a demand for
allotments, it is their duty to inquire and ascertain if suitable
land can be obtained for the purpose by voluntary arrangement at a reasonable rent and on reasonable conditions ;
and, if they find it cannot be so obtained, then they are empowered to purchase or hire any suitable land which may
be available either within or without their parish or district,
and to let such land in allotments not exceeding one acre,
to persons (men or women) belonging to the labouring
population resident in the parish or district.

7

By section 3, if suitable land cannot be purchased or hired by voluntary arrangement in sufficient quantity, the Local Authority may petition the County Council, and the County Council after due inquiry may make a Provisional Order compelling the owners to sell land for the purpose of allotments, under the provisions of what are known as the Lands Clauses Acts, and the Local Government Board are then empowered to introduce a Bill into Parliament to confirm the Provisional Order.[1]   The cost of a Provisional Order when not opposed is very small, amounting in most cases to only a few pounds.   Questions of disputed compensation for lands acquired by compulsory purchase are to be decided by a single arbitrator appointed by the parties, or, on application of either of them, by an arbitrator appointed by the Local Government Board, the remuneration of the arbitrator to be fixed by the Board.   With a view to prevent factious opposition, the arbitrator has power to disallow the costs of any witness, or any other costs which he considers have been unnecessarily incurred.

With the same object, it is, by section 4, provided that if a Provisional Order is opposed in Parliament, the Parliamentary Committee can order anyone to pay costs whose opposition they consider is not justified by the circumstances of the case.   Parks, gardens, pleasure grounds, lands used and required by Railway or Canal Companies, or for the convenience of dwelling-houses, cannot be taken by compulsory purchase; nor as far as it can possibly be avoided, is an undue or inconvenient quantity to be taken from any one owner.   Corporate bodies may lease lands to the Local Authority for the purpose of allotments for any term not exceeding thirty-five years.   (Section 3.)

---

[1] Under the Local Government Act, 1894, the procedure is somewhat altered,

By section 6, the Local Authority may make rules and regulations for managing the allotments, which must be confirmed by the Local Government Board, and a copy of these rules and regulations must be given gratis to any inhabitant applying for it. No undue preference, however, must be made in letting allotments, and no tenant is to be required to leave his tenancy without reasonable notice. As to what is "reasonable notice," the Local Government Board suggests that it shall be the same as that provided by the Agricultural Holdings Act, 1883, which is twelve months' notice expiring with a year of tenancy.

By sections 6 and 9, the Local Authority may appoint allotment managers to carry out the rules and regulations, but should the holders desire to elect their own managers, then, at a written request signed by not less than one-sixth of the electors in a parish, the Local Authority must arrange for the election of such managers; the election to be by ballot, and the number so elected to be not less than three or more than five.

By section 7, the rent of allotments is to be fixed at an amount not less than such as may be reasonably expected to secure the Local Authority (that is, the ratepayers) from loss. Subject to this, such rents may be from time to time charged as are reasonable, having regard to the value of similar land in the district.

By section 7, allotments must not be sub-let, and no one person can hold more than one acre (in addition to any common pasture land which may be provided under the Act) unless there are allotments vacant, in which case such allotments may be let to any person, but on condition that the Local Authority can resume possession within twelve months if the land is required for other persons who are without allotments. A tenant may erect on his allotment a tool-house, shed, green-house, fowl-house, or pig-sty, but no other buildings, and on quitting the holding he is at liberty to remove any such building he may have erected, or sell the same to an incoming tenant.

By section 8, if a tenant fail to pay his rent, or if he persistently violate the regulations for the management of allotments, or remove more than a mile outside the parish in which the allotments are situate, the Local Authority can, on due notice, determine his tenancy; provided that when a tenancy is thus determined, the Local Authority (in default of an agreement between the in-coming and out-going tenant) must, on demand, pay any compensation due to the tenant as an out-going tenant, the amount of such compensation to be assessed by an arbitrator appointed by the Local Authority, or—if the tenant so elect—by an arbitrator appointed under the Allotments and Cottage Gardens Compensation for Crops Act, 1887, or by a reference to the Agricultural Holdings Act, 1883. The tenant may also remove any fruit and other trees planted or acquired by him for which he may have no claim to compensation.

By section 10, all expenses incurred under the Act by the Local Authority are to be defrayed in accordance with the Public Health Act, 1875, and charged to the parish on account of which the land was acquired. And all sums received in respect of land so acquired (otherwise than from any sale or exchange) are to be applied in aid of the expenses in respect of such land, and any such surplus is to be credited to the parish on account of which the land was acquired. The Local Authority may borrow for the purpose of general and special expenses, and for acquiring, improving, and adapting land under this Act; the loans and the payment thereof to be under the provisions of the Public Health Act, 1875. Separate accounts of receipts and expenditure under the Act are to be kept and audited in the manner provided by the Act of 1875.

By section 11, the Authority may sell, let, or exchange any superfluous lands, and the proceeds must be applied in discharging, by way of a sinking fund or otherwise, the debts and liabilities in respect of acquiring land under the Act, or in acquiring, adapting, or improving other land for allotments. But all proceeds and surplus must be used for the benefit of the parish for which the land was acquired.

By section 12, in addition to land for allotments, the Local Authority are empowered to acquire land for common pasture, provided it can be acquired at a price which may reasonably be expected to be recouped by the rents ; and they are to make rules as to the persons who are to keep animals on the common pasture, the number to be kept, and the conditions and charges for each animal. It is therefore possible under the Act for a labourer to hold one acre of arable land and have also the right of common pasture.

Clause 13, sec. 2, contains a valuable provision. The Allotments Extension Act, 1882 (known as Mr. Jesse Collings' Act), provides that charity lands held for the benefit of the poor of a parish (except such lands be for educational, ecclesiastical, or apprenticeship purposes), shall be offered to labourers for allotments. The Act of 1882 has been largely used, but trustees are frequently unwilling to offer the land as required by the Act, lest the charity should suffer, or through trouble of collecting small rents ; and also because they have no money available for the purpose of preparing the land for allotments. These difficulties are overcome by this clause, which enables the trustees to sell or let the charity land in bulk to the Local Authority for the purposes of allotments, thereby relieving themselves from trouble, risk, and responsibility.

By section 14, two or more parishes may combine for the purposes of the Act, and any area other than a parish which is a contributory place under the Public Health Act, 1875, may also join.

It is important to note that in cases where the land has been acquired by the Local Authority by means of a loan repayable by instalments, the "expenses" referred to in section 2 of the Act (subsection 2) are to include the interest payable on the purchase money, but are not to include the instalments of principal, or payments to a sinking fund. The Authority is to pay all rates, taxes, and tithes, and is to fairly apportion the same among the allotment holders, and the sum so apportioned is to be added to and to be deemed part of the rent payable by the tenant. If the Authority think fit, they may require one quarter's rent in advance, but no more. Although the rates, taxes, and tithes are paid by the Authority, yet for the purposes of the Parliamentary franchise, and the municipal and other local franchises, the tenants are to be held as the occupiers.

THE ALLOTMENTS ACT, 1890.—The object of this short, simple, and useful Act is to provide for an appeal from Sanitary Authorities to County Councils when the former fail to acquire suitable allotments for the working men.

Where (section 2) the usual "representation" under the Allotments Act of 1887 has been made to the Sanitary Authority requiring them to enforce the provisions of that Act, and they have "failed to acquire land adequate and suitable in quality and position to provide a sufficient number of allotments," any six persons qualified to make such representation (*i.e.*, registered Parliamentary electors or ratepayers of the parish) may, under the Act of 1890,

petition the County Council, stating the facts, and requesting the Council to put into force the Act of 1887.
Persons who reside in boroughs and who may desire allotments have *no* such power of appeal or petition under this
or any other Act. The Council, if satisfied, after local
inquiry, that allotment land should be acquired, are to pass
a resolution to that effect, and thereupon the duties of the
Sanitary Authority under the Act of 1887, so far as regards
the land desired in the particular district or parish, become
transferred to the County Council. The County Council
must then proceed to acquire land in accordance with the
original Act of 1887.

Every County Council is, by section 3, required annually
at the meeting for the election of chairman, to appoint an
allotments committee, not exceeding one-fourth of the
whole number of members of the Council; and to this
committee all allotment petitions under the Act to the
County Council are to be referred by that body as a matter
of course. The County Councillor of a district or parish
situate wholly or partly in an electoral division where allotments are desired, is to be an additional member of the
said committee if not already appointed. The committee,
on being satisfied as to the bonâ-fide character of any
petition, is immediately to make a local inquiry into the
circumstances, and to report the result to the Council.
Such inquiry may be held by one or more members of the
committee, or by such other person as the committee may
appoint.

By section 4 it is provided that if the duty or powers
of the Sanitary Authority under the Act of 1887 become
transferred to the County Council, the following provisions are to have effect:—(*a*) The Act of 1887 is to apply
with the modifications necessary for giving effect to the

Allotments Appeals Act, 1890. (*b*) The County Council may borrow money in the same way and on the same security as the Sanitary Authority under the Act of 1887 are empowered to do; and the Sanitary Authority are to repay the borrowed money and interest, as if the same had been raised by the said Authority themselves. (*c*) The County Council are to keep separate accounts of all receipts and expenditure. (*d*) The County Council may make a Provisional Order for the compulsory purchase of land on the recommendation of the standing committee, without any petition from the Sanitary Authority; and the Council are to be considered as the promoters of the Order. (*e*) The County Council may delegate to the Sanitary Authority any powers under sections 6, 7, or 8 of the Act of 1887 (which relate to the management of allotments, the letting and use thereof, and the recovery of rent and possession). Subject to the terms of the delegation, all expenses and receipts arising out of the exercise of the duties so delegated are to be paid and dealt with as under the Act of 1887. (*f*) The County Council, at the request of the Sanitary Authority, may transfer to the latter all or any of their (the Council's) powers, etc., under the Act of 1890 as regards the district of the said Sanitary Authority or any part of it.

Section 5 says that the free use of any room in a school receiving public funds may, subject to six days' notice, be had (except during school hours) for the purposes of the Act of 1890 by the County Council; or, with the consent of any two managers, the free use of any such school may be had in order to discuss any question under the Acts of 1887 or 1890. Any damage done to the room or any expense incurred is to be paid by the County Council or by the persons calling the meeting. Those local inhabitants signing the notice must not be less than six in number, and

they must be registered Parliamentary electors or ratepayers of the parish in which the allotments are desired.
The notice must be sent or given to the clerk of the Board
if the school is under a School Board; and in any other
case, to one of the managers of the school. If, however,
the use of the schoolroom for the time fixed for the meeting has, previously to the receipt of the notice, been
granted for some other purpose, the notice is void, although
in that case an intimation of such previous use having been
granted must immediately, on receipt of the notice, be
made to one of the persons signing it, together with an intimation naming some other day on which the room may
be used. In case the persons calling the meeting fail to
obtain the use of the room, they may appeal to the standing committee before mentioned, and the committee is
forthwith to decide the appeal, and to make such order
respecting the use of the room as seems just.

By section 6 (the last in the enactment) provision is
made for the payment of the expenses incurred. In certain
events these are to be thrown upon the defaulting Sanitary
Authority.

THE LOCAL GOVERNMENT ACT, 1894.—Under the Local
Government Act, 1894, the procedure in acquiring allotments under the Allotments Acts of 1887 and 1890, has
been what we may term "modified" in part and added to
in part. The various clauses in the Act which relate to allotments may as well, in view of the great public interest
which has been manifested in them, be given exactly as
they stand in the measure. They are as follows :—

Section 6, subsection (3), says :—" A Parish Council shall have the
same power of making a representation with respect to allotments, and
of applying for the election of allotment managers, as is conferred on
Parliamentary electors by the Allotments Act, 1887, or the Allot-

ments Act, 1890, but without prejudice to the powers of those electors."

Subsection (4) declares :—" Where any Act constitutes any persons wardens for allotments, or authorises or requires the appointment or election of any wardens, committee or managers for the purpose of allotments, then, after a Parish Council for the parish interested in such allotments comes into office, the powers and duties of the wardens, committee, or managers shall be exercised and performed by the Parish Council, and it shall not be necessary to make the said appointment or to hold the said election, and for the purpose of section sixteen of the Small Holdings Act, 1892, two members of the Parish Council shall be substituted for allotment managers or persons appointed as allotment managers."

Section 9 and its various important subsections are :—"(1) For the purpose of the acquisition of land by a Parish Council, the Lands Clauses Acts shall be incorporated with this Act, except the provisions of those Acts with respect to the purchase and taking of land otherwise than by agreement, and section one hundred and seventy-eight of the Public Health Act, 1875, shall apply as if the Parish Council were referred to therein. (2) If a Parish Council are unable to acquire by agreement and on reasonable terms suitable land for any purpose for which they are authorised to acquire it, they may represent the case to the County Council, and the County Council shall inquire into the representation. (3) If on any such representation, or on any proceeding under the Allotments Acts, 1887 and 1890, a County Council are satisfied that suitable land for the said purpose of the Parish Council or for the purpose of allotments (as the case may be), cannot be acquired on reasonable terms by voluntary agreement, and that the circumstances are such as to justify the County Council in proceeding under this section (*i.e.* section 9), they shall cause such public inquiry to be made in the parish, and such notice to be given both in the parish and to the owners, lessees, and occupiers of the land proposed to be taken, as may be prescribed, and all persons interested shall be permitted to attend at the inquiry, and to support or oppose the taking of the land. (4) After the completion of the inquiry, and considering all objections made by any persons interested, the County Council may make an order for putting in force, as respects the said land or any part thereof, the provisions of the Lands Clauses Acts with respect to the purchase and taking of land otherwise than by agreement. (5) If the County

Council refuse to make any such order, the Parish Council, or, if the proceeding is taken on the petition of the District Council, then the District Council may petition the Local Government Board, and that Board after local inquiry may, if they think proper, make the order, and this section shall apply as if the order had been made by the County Council. Any order made under this subsection overruling the decision of the County Council shall be laid before Parliament by the Local Government Board. (6) A copy of any order made under this section shall be served in the prescribed manner, together with a statement that the order will become final and have the effect of an Act of Parliament, unless within the prescribed period a memorial by some person interested is presented to the Local Government Board praying that the order shall not become law without further inquiry. (7) The order shall be deposited with the Local Government Board, who shall inquire whether the provisions of this section and the prescribed regulations have been in all respects complied with ; and if the Board are satisfied that this has been done, then, after the prescribed period—(a) If no memorial has been presented, or if every such memorial has been withdrawn, the Board shall, without further inquiry, confirm the order : (b) If a memorial has been presented, the Local Government Board shall proceed to hold a local inquiry, and shall, after such inquiry, either confirm, with or without amendment, or disallow the order : (c) Upon any such confirmation the order, and if amended as so amended, shall become final and have the effect of an Act of Parliament, and the confirmation by the Local Government Board shall be conclusive evidence that the requirements of this Act have been complied with, and that the order has been duly made, and is within the powers of this Act. (8) Sections two hundred and ninety-three to two hundred and ninety-six, and subsections (1) and (2) of section two hundred and ninety-seven of the Public Health Act, 1875, shall apply to a local inquiry held by the Local Government Board for the purposes of this section, as if those sections and subsections were herein re-enacted, and in terms made applicable to such inquiry. (9) The order shall be carried into effect, when made on the petition of a District Council, by that council, and in any other case by the County Council. (10) Any order made under this section for the purpose of the purchase of land otherwise than by agreement shall incorporate the Lands Clauses Acts and sections seventy-seven to eighty-five of the Railways Clauses Consolidation Act, 1845, with the necessary adaptations, but any question of disputed com-

B

pensation shall be dealt with in the manner provided by section three of the Allotments Act, 1887, and provisoes (*a*), (*b*), and (*c*) of subsection (4) of that section are incorporated with this section and shall apply accordingly : Provided that in determining the amount of disputed compensation, the arbitrator shall not make any additional allowance in respect of the purchase being compulsory.   (11) At any inquiry or arbitration held under this section the person or persons holding the inquiry or arbitration shall hear any authorities or parties interested, by themselves or their agents, and shall hear witnesses, but shall not, except in such cases as may be prescribed, hear counsel or expert witnesses.   (12) The person or persons holding a public inquiry for the purposes of this section on behalf of a County Council shall have the same powers as an inspector or inspectors of the Local Government Board when holding a local inquiry ; and section two hundred and ninety-four of the Public Health Act, 1875, shall apply to the costs of inquiries held by the County Council for the purpose of this section as if the County Council were substituted for the Local Government Board. (13) Subsection (2) of section two, if the land is taken for allotments, and, whether it is or is not so taken, subsections (5), (6), (7), and (8) of section three of the Allotments Act, 1887, and section eleven of that Act, and section three of the Allotments Act, 1890, are incorporated with this section, and shall, with the prescribed adaptations, apply accordingly.   (14) Where the land is acquired otherwise than for allotments, it shall be assured to the Parish Council ; and any land purchased by a County Council for allotments under the Allotments Acts, 1887 and 1890, and this Act, or any of them, shall be assured to the Parish Council, and in that case sections five to eight of the Allotments Act, 1887, shall apply as if the Parish Council were the Sanitary Authority.   (15) Nothing in this section shall authorise the Parish Council to acquire otherwise than by agreement any land for the purpose of any supply of water, or of any right of way.   (16) In this section the expression "allotments" includes common pasture where authorised to be acquired under the Allotments Act, 1887.   (17) Where, under the Allotments Act, 1890, the Allotments Act, 1887, applies to the purchase of land by the County Council, that Act shall apply as amended by this section ; and the Parish Council shall have the like power of petitioning the County Council as is given to six parliamentary electors by section two of the Allotments Act, 1890.   (18) This section shall apply to a County Borough with the necessary modifications, and in particular with the modification that the order shall be both made and confirmed by the Local Government Board, and shall be carried into effect by the Council of the County Borough. (19) The expenses of a County Council incurred under this section shall be defrayed in like manner as in the case of a local inquiry by a County Council under this Act."

Section 10 and its subsections, for the first time, permit of the compulsory *hiring* of land for allotment purposes, and are :—" (1) The Parish Council shall have power to hire land for allotments, and if they are satisfied that allotments are required, and are unable to hire by agreement on reasonable terms suitable land for allotments, they shall represent the case to the County Council, and the County Council may make an order authorising the Parish Council to hire compulsorily for allotments, for a period not less than fourteen years nor more than thirty-five years, such land in or near the parish as is specified in the order, and the order shall, as respects confirmation and otherwise, be subject to the like provisions as if it were an order of the County Council made under the last preceding section (*i.e.*, section 9) of this Act, and that section shall apply as if it were herein re-enacted with the substitution of ' hiring ' for ' purchase ' and with the other necessary modifications. (2) A single arbitrator, who shall be appointed in accordance with the provisions of section three of the Allotments Act, 1887, and to whom the provisions of that section shall apply, shall have power to determine any question—(a) as to the terms and conditions of the hiring ; or (b) as to the amount of compensation for severance ; or (c) as to the compensation to any tenant upon the determination of his tenancy ; or (d) as to the apportionment of the rent between the land taken by the Parish Council and the land not taken from the tenant ; or (e) as to any other matter incidental to the hiring of the land by the Council, or the surrender thereof at the end of their tenancy ; but the arbitrator in fixing the rent shall not make any addition in respect of compulsory hiring. (3) The arbitrator, in fixing rent or other compensation, shall take into consideration all the circumstances connected with the land, and the use to which it might otherwise be put by the owner during the term of hiring, and any depreciation of the value to the tenant of the residue of his holding caused by the withdrawal from the holding of the land hired by the Parish Council. (4) Any compensation awarded to a tenant in respect of any depreciation of the value to him of the residue of his holding caused by the withdrawal from the holding of the land hired by the Parish Council shall as far as possible be provided for by taking such compensation into account in fixing, as the case may require, the rent to be paid by the Parish Council for the land hired by them, and the apportioned rent, if any, to be paid by the tenant for that portion of the holding which is not hired by the Parish Council. (5) The award of the arbitrator or a copy thereof, together with a report signed by him as to the condition of the land taken by the Parish Council, shall be deposited and preserved with the public books, writings, and papers of the Parish, and the owner for the time being of the land shall at all reasonable times be at liberty to inspect the same and to take copies thereot. (6) Save as hereinafter mentioned, sections five to eight of the Allotments Act, 1887, shall apply to any allotment hired by a Parish Council in like manner as if that Council were the Sanitary Authority and also the allotment managers : Provided that the Parish Council—(a) may let to one person an allotment or allotments exceeding one acre, but, if the land is hired compulsorily, not exceeding in the whole four acres of pasture or one acre of arable and three acres of pasture ; and (b) may permit to be erected on the allotment any stable, cowhouse, or barn ; and (c) shall not break up, or permit to be broken up, any permanent pasture, without the assent in writing of the landlord. (7) On the determination of any tenancy created by compulsory hiring, a single arbitrator who shall be appointed in accordance with the provisions of section three of the Allotments Act, 1887, shall have power to determine as to the amount due by the landlord for compensation for improvements, or by the Parish Council for depreciation, but such compensation shall be assessed in accordance with the provisions of the Agricultural Holdings (England) Act, 1883. (8) The order for compulsory hiring may apply, with the prescribed adaptations, to such of the provisions of the Lands Clauses Acts (including those relating to the acquisition of land otherwise than by agreement) as appear to the County Council or Local Government Board sufficient for carrying into effect the order, and for the protection of the persons interested in the land and of the Parish Council. (9) Nothing in this section shall authorise the compulsory hiring of any mines or minerals, or confer any right to take, sell, or carry away any gravel, sand, or clay, or authorise the hiring of any land which is already owned or occupied as a small holding within the meaning of the Small Holdings Act, 1892. (10) If the land hired under this section shall at any time during the tenancy thereof by the Parish Council be shown to the satisfaction of the County Council to be required by the landlord for the purpose of working and getting the mines, minerals, or surface minerals thereunder, or for any road or work to be used in connexion with such working or getting, it shall be lawful for the landlord of such land to resume possession thereof upon giving to the Parish Council twelve calendar months previous notice in writing of his intention so to do, and upon such resumption the landlord shall pay to the Parish Council and to the allotment holders of the land for the time being such sum by way of compensation for the loss of such land for the purposes of allotments as may be agreed upon by the landlord and the Parish Council, or in default of such agreement as may be awarded by a single arbitrator to be appointed in accordance with the provisions of section three of the Allotments Act, 1887, and the provisions of that section shall apply to such arbitrator. The word 'landlord' in this subsection means the person for the time being entitled to receive the rent of the land hired by the Parish Council. (11) The Local Government Board shall annually lay before Parliament a report of any proceedings under this and the preceding section."

With regard to the expenses of a Parish Council in acquiring allotments we may as well quote what the Act says concerning expenses generally. Section 11 declares :—" (1) A Parish Council shall not, without the consent of a Parish Meeting, incur expenses or liabilities which will involve a rate exceeding *threepence* in the pound for any local financial year, or which will involve a loan. (2) A Parish Council shall not, without the approval of the County Council, incur any expense or liability which will *involve a loan.* (3) The sum raised in any local financial year by a Parish Council for their expenses, other than expenses under the Adoptive Acts [to acquire allotments does *not* come under the 'Adoptive Acts'], shall not exceed a sum equal to a rate of *sixpence in the pound* on the rateable value of the parish at the commencement of the year, and for the purpose of this enactment the expression 'expenses' includes any annual charge, whether of principal or interest, in respect of any loan."

In comparing the Local Government Act, 1894, with the Allotments Acts, 1887 and 1890, the following should be borne in mind :—

1. It is not now necessary to obtain the consent of Parliament when allotment land is acquired compulsorily from an owner.

2. The County Council, or in the event of an appeal, the Local Government Board, have alone the power to take land compulsorily for allotment purposes.

3. A tenant may in certain circumstances (see section 10, subsection 6) have as many as four acres for allotments.

4. Rural residents who desire allotments but who have not a Parish Council must (as previous to the passing of the Local Government Act, 1894) apply for them to the Sanitary Authority (now the District Council) under the Allotments Act, 1887 : unless the Parish Meeting choose to apply to the County Council, and the County Council then confer on the Parish Meeting such of the powers of a Parish Council as in the matter of allotments the said meeting may ask for or desire. Any such application, however, would probably involve a great deal of unnecessary delay.

5. It has been urged that under the Local Government Act, 1894, the persons entitled to allotments are the "labouring population." As to the meaning of the term "labouring population," the law officers of the Crown say that the expression means the population that, in substance, makes a living by manual labour, and that it includes all such as smiths, ploughmen, carpenters, artificers, workers in factories, and others whose work is in the main manual, though knowledge and skill also be required ; but that it does not include those whose work is in the main a matter of knowledge and skill, though manual labour also be required, such as nurses or cooks, postmasters, clerks, or tradesmen. In general the law officers consider that the line of demarcation is that above indicated, but that it is

impossible to lay it down with precision, and that each case must depend on its facts. Further, they observe that section 2 of the Allotments Act, 1887, authorises the letting of allotments to " persons belonging to the labouring population," and the expression, in the opinion of the law officers, includes not only those who labour themselves, but those really belonging to the class, though personally they may not labour; for example, the widow of a labourer.

But we may add a few words to what the law officers have stated. The term "labouring population" has been very narrowly construed in some cases. When the Allotments Bill was before Parliament in 1887, it was felt that some term must be inserted in it in order that the measure might not be unnecessarily cramped or restricted. To have inserted "agricultural" labouring population, or "artisan" population, or even both, would have been a grave mistake, as the slightest reflection will show. The measure was certainly never intended for either one alone of those "classes." On the other hand, the term "labouring" population cannot, if we bear in mind the whole spirit in which the Allotments Bill was conceived, debated, and passed into an Act, be open to serious objection. Our own opinion is that any and every man or woman who earns his or her livelihood largely or chiefly by manual work comes well within the meaning of the term, and is, in point of fact, a "labourer" in the best and just sense of the term. Obviously, if any great number of those were *excluded* whom we here argue should be *included*, the Allotments Act would be a nullity in many thousands of cases where it is needed, and where, too, it is most likely to prove advantageous. Our view, however, is backed up by Mr. Ritchie (President of the Local Government Board in the Parliament which passed the Allotments Act), as well as by the Allotments Provisional Order Confirmation Act, 1891, and by the Cheshire Lines Committee Act, 1893. In the Act of 1891 alluded to, the term is distinctly made to include "mechanics, artizans, labourers, and others working for wages; hawkers, costermongers, persons not working for wages, but working at some trade or handicraft without employing others except members of their own family; and persons, other than domestic servants, whose income does not exceed an average of thirty shillings a week, and the families of any of such persons who may be residing with them." In the Act of 1893 exactly the same significance is given to the term. The Allotments Act, 1887, has therefore a wider significance than the Local Government Act, 1894, and would no doubt include rural postmasters, tradesmen, etc., and women (whether widows or not).

CHAPTER III.

IF an individual desire an allotment he should first apply to the owner of the land to see if he be willing to grant it to him. In rural districts it may often be found more convenient to apply to the tenant (usually a farmer); this is not the legal method, but to do so may obviate any feeling of soreness at going otherwise behind the farmer's back, *i.e.,* to his landlord. If the farmer consent, the landlord will, in nine cases of ten, do so too; at all events, such is our experience.

If the land cannot be obtained by voluntary means from one owner in the district, then application should be made in turn to the other owners (if there are any) having suitable land.

Should none then be secured, formal application should be made either to the Sanitary Authority (*i.e.,* the District Council) for the locality where the allotments are wanted, or to the Parish Council.

To enable this and other formal applications to be made, we have drawn up several petitions. These may be copied out, and when filled in, should be sent to the Clerk to the District Council, or to the Parish Council, or County Council, as the case may be.

We have also drawn up other petitions for use by Parish Councils who may either wish (1) to act on being formally asked by applicants to do so; or (2) to take the initiative themselves in the matter.

25

(1) PETITION TO THE SANITARY AUTHORITY (NOW THE DISTRICT COUNCIL), BY ELECTORS OR RATEPAYERS.

THE ALLOTMENTS ACTS, 1887 AND 1890 : AND THE LOCAL GOVERNMENT ACT, 1894.

To the Sanitary Authority for the Union of ———

GENTLEMEN,

As registered Parliamentary electors or ratepayers, residing in the parish of ———, we hereby represent to your Authority that there is a demand for allotments for the labouring population of the said place, and that it is impossible to obtain such allotments by voluntary arrangements between the owners of suitable land and the applicants for the same.

Name.	Address.	Quantity of land required by each applicant.

(2) PETITION TO COUNTY COUNCIL BY ELECTORS OR RATEPAYERS AFTER FAILURE OF SANITARY AUTHORITY TO PROVIDE LAND.

ALLOTMENTS ACTS, 1887 AND 1890 : AND THE LOCAL GOVERNMENT ACT, 1894.

To the County Council for———

GENTLEMEN,

As registered Parliamentary electors or ratepayers residing in the parish of ———, we hereby represent to your Council (1) That under section 2, subsection 1, of the Allotments Act, 1887, a representation was made to the Sanitary Authority for the ——— Union, on the ——— day of ——— 189— ; (2) That it is the duty of the said Sanitary Authority to take proceedings under that Act therein ; and (3) That the said Sanitary Authority have failed to acquire any land for allotments for the parish.

We, therefore, respectfully ask that your Council may put into operation the above Acts for the purpose of providing a sufficient number of suitable allotments for the said parish.

Name.	Address.	Quantity of land desired by each applicant.

(3) PETITION BY PARISHIONERS TO PARISH COUNCIL TO ACQUIRE ALLOTMENTS.

THE LOCAL GOVERNMENT ACT, 1894.

To the Parish ———— Council.

GENTLEMEN,

We, the undersigned, respectfully request that allotment land may be provided for us under the above Act.

Name.	Address.	Quantity of land required by each applicant.

(4) PETITION TO A DISTRICT COUNCIL BY A PARISH COUNCIL.

THE LOCAL GOVERNMENT ACT, 1894 : AND THE ALLOTMENTS ACTS, 1887 AND 1890.

To the ———— District Council.

GENTLEMEN,

At a meeting of the ———— Parish Council held on the ———— day of ————, 189—, at which there was a quorum of members present, I was requested to represent, and I do hereby represent, to the ———— District Council, that there is a demand in the said parish for allotments under the above Acts ; and that such allotments cannot be obtained by volun-

tary arrangement between the owners of suitable land and the ——
Parish Council.

Name,...................................

[Here state whether Clerk or Chairman of the ——— Parish Council.]

Address,.. ....

....

(5) PETITION BY A PARISH COUNCIL TO A COUNTY COUNCIL ON A DISTRICT COUNCIL FAILING TO PROVIDE LAND.

THE LOCAL GOVERNMENT ACT, 1894: AND THE ALLOTMENTS ACTS, 1887 AND 1890.

To the County Council for ———.

GENTLEMEN,

At a meeting of the ———Parish Council held on the ——— day of ———, 189—, at which there was a quorum of members present, I was requested to represent, and I do hereby represent, to you (1) That, under section 2, subsection 1, of the Allotments Act, 1887, a representation was made to the——District Council on the——day of———, 189—; (2) That it is the duty of the said District Council to take proceedings under that Act therein; and (3) That the said District Council have failed to acquire any land for allotments for the said parish. It was also resolved that I should request, and I do hereby request, the County Council to put into force the above Acts, for the purpose of providing a sufficient number of suitable allotments for the said parish. The total quantity desired is ——— acres.

Name,...... ....

[Here state whether Clerk or Chairman of the ——— Parish Council.]

Address,...................................

....

(6) PETITION BY A PARISH COUNCIL TO A COUNTY COUNCIL TO COMPULSORILY HIRE LAND.

THE LOCAL GOVERNMENT ACT, 1894: AND THE ALLOTMENTS ACT, 1887.

To the County Council for ———

GENTLEMEN,

At a meeting of the ——— Parish Council held on the ·——— day of ———, 189—, at which there was a quorum of members present, I was requested to represent, and I do hereby represent, to you, that there is a demand for allotments under section 10 of the Local Government Act, 1894, in the parish of ———, and that suitable land for such allotments cannot be hired by voluntary agreement on reasonable terms. It was also resolved that I should request, and I do hereby request, your Council to put in force the compulsory provisions of section 10 of the Local Government Act of 1894, with the view of providing suitable land for allotment purposes under that section to satisfy the said demand. The total quantity of land desired is ——— acres.

Name,.....................................

[Here state whether Clerk or Chairman of the ——— Parish Council.]

Address,............. ....

....

CHAPTER IV.

"ACREAGE" AND RESULTS.

THERE are those, and especially farmers, who are of opinion that so long as the labourer is in the receipt of a regular wage, allotments are quite beside the question, useless, and therefore unnecessary. To talk thus is to place a barrier across the legitimate path of progress of the humble cultivator in question; and we venture to think there can be but few persons who, if the tables were reversed, would entertain the same idea on the subject.

Admitting, as we think all reasonable persons must do, the desirability of allotments for the rural working classes, it becomes a matter of importance that the land which a holder desires to cultivate should be neither too far from his dwelling nor too large for his opportunities. It may fairly be urged that an allotment should not be so large as to interfere with the labour required by the farmer who engages the service of the allotment holder. Subject to this observation it is very difficult to limit the exact size. We know of a large number of labourers who started with $\frac{1}{2}$-acre plots, but who had to give them up as being too small. They were then allowed to have 1-acre plots each, and are doing remarkably well with them. On the other hand we have known far more numerous instances where the quantity of land with which the men started had to be reduced either at their own request or because it was perfectly manifest to

30

the owners that they had taken more than that to which
they could do justice.

Now suppose a man had an allotment of one acre. One-
fourth or one-third might very well be put down to wheat.
This would go a long way towards providing his family with
bread, and would revive the habit of bread-making, which
was once general in all rural parishes. We know of an
allotment of one quarter of an acre which produced, last
harvest, between two and three quarters of wheat and half a
ton of straw—which is nearly four times the average production. Wheat is a crop which requires comparatively little
labour, and we think labourers would do well in appropriating
a good portion of their allotments to it; they would always find
it a profitable crop. If the labourer has a family his children
should (according to Mr. J. C. Buckmaster) *dibble in* the seed,
which would save seed, and give a much better yield. The
weeding in spring would be a light and pleasant occupation
for the family. The seed should be put in as early as possible
after harvest. Sown in the autumn, it is more productive
than when sown in the spring. If a man has a pig, barley
is a profitable crop; and potatoes, peas, beans, turnips,
kohl rabi, carrots, onions, cabbages, and other vegetables,
should be grown, as may be best suited to the natural capa-
bilities of the soil. If the land be wet and heavy, the first
thing to consider is drainage. We know of allotments that
suffer very much from want of drainage. We should re-
commend no man to take land that wants draining. As far
as possible the allotment should be cultivated with a spade
or digger, and kept as free from weeds as a well managed
garden. It should always be borne in mind that every weed
takes something from the land which ought to feed more
profitable plants. Another very important matter, but
often disregarded, is the selection of seed. Good advice

on this point may often be obtained from neighbours. A difficulty of the allotment system, however, is concerning the necessary supply of manure, and without plenty of manure, profitable cultivation is not possible. Farmyard manure is out of the question in many cases, and is everywhere a diminishing quantity. The quantity obtained by keeping a pig, and the use even of household garbage, etc., is not always sufficient. Artificial manures may, therefore, supplement natural manures. All the fertilising property of farmyard manure may be obtained from artificials; and here comes the necessity for that kind of knowledge called "science." There are four important constituents in all manures—nitrogen, zinc, potash, and bones, or superphosphates; with these we may grow almost anything. No hard and fast rule can be applied to the proper use of manures. Everything depends on knowledge, and side by side with the allotment system there should grow up a sound system of technical instruction in agricultural and horticultural practice.

As to the monetary returns from the cultivation of allotments, we may quote the following instance (one of many to the same effect), the particulars of which were supplied to us by the occupier himself. He said that after paying for a considerable portion of the labour incidental to a plot of twenty-six perches, he found, at the end of the season, that his "returns" covered all expenses, rent included, leaving a balance of four sacks of potatoes, and sufficient greenstuff to last through the winter; and this, taking no account of the produce consumed by his household during the whole of the summer. There could, he said, be no room for the question, "Will it pay?" And he went on to observe: "The truth is, and I do not exaggerate in asserting it, that it can be made to pay fifty per cent.; and those, therefore, who invest in the Savings Bank, at three per cent., or less, and could manage an allotment, had better re-consider their policy.   Should this, however, be doubted, let the cost and production severally, of twenty perches of ground, be estimated, and the judgment of experienced hands be taken upon it, when the doubt will be somewhat dispelled.   Take twenty perches of potatoes and we have the following result :—

	£	s.	d.
Rent, 8d. per perch	0	13	4
Seed, 20 quarterns of 10 lbs. each ...	0	10	0
Manure, 4 loads at 2s. 2d. each... ...	0	8	8
Digging, 4d. per perch, usual price ...	0	6	8
Hoeing, at 3s. 4d. per day	0	6	8
Planting	0	3	4
Digging, sacking, and carting	0	8	2
	2	16	10
Produce, 10 sacks at 8s.	4	0	0
Balance to the good	£1	3	2

" This is for but one crop, which no experienced ' hand ' would be satisfied with, but would farm for two, and would estimate the winter crop at little less value than that of the summer."

A question which has often caused a good deal of wonderment to many persons is, How does the labourer with a wife and family manage to eke out a living, even supposing that he has the advantages which an allotment, properly cultivated, affords? We confess we have, over and over again, put this question to ourselves, and that, with much experience of the rural labouring class, the wonderment

c

still remains with us. However, an actual instance of
" how it is done," will afford a good deal more interest,
instruction, and satisfaction, than any mere pious specula-
tion on the subject. We refer to a certain Berkshire
labourer, a carter. This man has a cottage and garden and
15s. a week. His eldest boy, aged fourteen, who left school
at thirteen, has 6s. a week, as helper in a gentleman's
stable not far off. There are six other children. Here,
then, is a labourer and his family under very favourable
conditions. A cottage and garden, 21s. a week " coming
in," the parents being sober, industrious, *good-living* people,
the children well brought up, and giving as little trouble as
children can. Well, how do such people as these spend
their money, and how much can they put by for old age
out of the week's wages ? Let us have a talk with the good
wife, and she will tell us. We knock at the door, and
we soon find ourselves in her house. "Mrs. C——," we
say, " we have come to have ten minutes' chat, so sit down
in peace for that time and talk to us." We help ourselves
to a chair, and the woman takes another on the other side
of the fire. A child of a year old, seeing its mother sitting
down, crawls towards her and cries to be taken on her
knee. As soon as it has got into the coveted place another
child of two or three comes toddling up, demanding to
be taken up also. This we lift on our own knee. A child
who has been playing all the afternoon on a brick floor
cannot be lifted on to one's dark cloth clothes without a
twinge of dismay. But the little thing's proud and contented look as it sits on our knee soon makes us for-
get such considerations. Poor people's children, when
there are seven in a family, don't often get nursed, and this
child, with a knee all to himself, and a strong hand round
his back, and his little toes toasting before the fire, is in the

enjoyment for the moment of a happiness which a child of a princely house could hardly ever know.

"Well, Mrs. C——, how have you been getting on ? " Mrs. C—— says she has been feeling very worn and tired. When we ask her what has thrown extra work on her, she says, "The work has been much as usual, but I've been living extra hard. I've bought a new suit for Edward for Sunday for 22s. 6d. I can't pinch the children to pay for them, so I've had to go without myself."

We said that we thought that since her boy had got to work, and was adding 6s. to the family income every week, we had hoped she would have been in comparatively easy circumstances. "It does make a deal of difference," she says ; " of course, he eats more and wears out more clothes, but it's not as dreadful as it was when I had to do all on 15s. I have to buy a pair of boots every fortnight. The children have half-a-mile to go to school, and they must be well shod. Their shoes cost me 3s. 6d. a pair, one with another. The husband's come heavier, but they last longer."

We suggested, with a smile, that she had not said anything about the cost of her own boots.

"Oh," she said, "I can't afford to think of myself."

" But," we said, " you must be clothed ; how did you buy that dress you have on ? "

"This," she replied, "was given me by my sister, who is in service. She had done with it, and gave it me five years ago. I have worn it for every-day ever since. I have unpicked it, and turned it twice in the time."

"Come, Mrs. C——," we said, "we cannot make out how things can be as bad with you as all that. Do you mind telling us how you spend your week's money ? "

We took down from her lips the following account of her weekly expenditure :—

					s.	d.
Bread	...	...	...	...	7	9
Butter, 2 lbs.	...	...	...	...	2	2
Tea, ½ lb.	...	..	...	...	1	0
Sugar, 6 lbs. at 2½d.	...	...	..		1	3
Coals	...	...	..	...	2	0
Clothing (including 6d. a week to the Clothing Club)	...	...	...	..	2	6
Sick Club, for husband and eldest boy		...			0	8
Boots, for children and husband	...		...		2	0
Rice, treacle, suet, etc.	...	...	...		0	6
Soap, soda, starch, washing-flannel, and scrubbing-brushes ...	...	...	...		0	6
Bacon	...	...	...	...	1	5
			Total	..	£1 1	9

"Why," we said, "this is 9d. more than your income. Where do you get the 9d. from ? "

"Sometimes," she said, "I make a few pence by doing a little needlework for a neighbour. But it's very hard to keep out of debt. The worst of all is the doctor. If we have him for one of the children, it seems as if we must give up trying any longer, for it's next to impossible to find the money to pay him."

"Whose turn is it next," we said, "for a new pair of boots ? "

" Jim's ; his father has mended them two or three times, but they won't keep the water out, and are not fit for going to school on wet days."

"Well," we said, "we'll stand a pair of new boots for Jim, and then you can add a bit of butcher's meat to his Sunday's dinner ! "

In this account nothing has been said about the man's garden close at his door, and supplying fresh vegetables, which just turn the balance against the hard living and enable the children to get food sufficient in quantity and variety to make the necessary bone and tissue required for healthy growth. The children are as bright and happy as any children could be in any class of life. The necessity for continual effort in such a family bears its good fruit ; habits of industry are formed, and the sense of responsibility, and the call which comes to each at a very early age to bear a hand to keep the family ship afloat, give these children an advantage in the struggles of life over those who are nursed in luxury, which, but for their inferior education, would often make them the winners in the race.

But who can wonder if some of our rural labourers, under harder circumstances than those that have been described, turn their backs and fly from the battle, seeking the fatal solace of the public-house and ending their days in the union workhouse, or quite as badly in a distant town ?

CHAPTER V.

THANKS to allotments undoubtedly becoming more common, the comparative comfort of the allottee's home is also of a higher order.

Out of this state of things "Allotment Societies," "Pig Clubs," "Cow Clubs," and similar institutions are taking root; and where we have had an opportunity for inquiry and observation regarding them, they have proved, and are proving, of the utmost value. In the formation of the rules of some of these societies, etc., it has been our very pleasant lot to take part : and in the hope that the details may be useful in other localities, we venture to give specimens of such rules, which can, however, be varied somewhat to meet local requirements.

RULES OF A CO-OPERATIVE ALLOTMENT SOCIETY.

The following rules are of a Co-operative Allotment Society, which society and rules have been duly approved and registered in accordance with the law. The rules are of special value as being those of a Co-operative Land Society, the like of which, we believe, does not exist anywhere in this country, but in the one district to which the rules especially refer :—

1.—The Society is a specially authorised Society, composed of members over sixteen years of age, and established under the special authority of March 23rd, 1877, for promoting agriculture and horti-culture.

2.—The Society shall be called the " —— Co-operative Allot-ment Society." Its registered office is in England, and is —— —— in the county of ——. In the event of any change in the situation of the registered office, notice of such change shall be sent within fourteen days thereafter to the Registrar in the form prescribed by the Treasury Regulations in that behalf.

3.—This Society is established to provide, by voluntary subscrip-tion of the members, for the promotion of agriculture or horticulture on allotments and lands in the parish of —— aforesaid.

4.—All money received on account of contributions, donations, admissions, fines or otherwise, shall be applied towards carrying out the object of the Society according to the rules thereof. Any officer mis-applying the funds shall repay the same and be excluded without prejudice to his liability to prosecution for such mis-application.

5.—All holders of land held by the Society for small holdings and allotments shall be taken to be members of the Society. But member-ship shall not be conferred by the tenancy of any buildings or lands let by the Society at a fixed rent and expressly stated to be not under these rules.

6.—All applications for Holdings shall be addressed in writing to the Secretary at the Registered office of the Society, and shall be brought before the Committee at their usual meetings. The decision of the Committee upon the application shall be final.

7.—All rents shall be determined by the Committee.

8.—All rents shall be paid to the Treasurer and Secretary of the Committee, by whom an account thereof shall be rendered to the Committee.

9.—All rents shall be paid quarterly in advance upon the usual quarter days, *i.e.*, September 29th, December 25th, March 25th, June 24th, and shall be deemed due and payable on those days.

10.—Any member who shall not make his payment at the time it shall be due, shall be deemed to have infringed the rules of the Society, and if such rent shall not be paid within fourteen days, he shall cease to be a member, and his tenancy shall at once terminate.

11.—All such rents, together with the rents of all buildings and lands let therewith held by the Society, shall be termed the " Common Fund " to be devoted to the payment of the rent due to the owners of the soil, of rates, taxes, repairs, and cost of management.

12.—If from such " Common Fund " after such payments shall have been made there shall at the end of each year remain a surplus, then shall such surplus or so much of such surplus as is thought desir-able by the Committee, be divided among the members according to the amount of land held.

13.—If such Common Fund be found to be insufficient for such payments, then shall such contribution be required of the members *pro rata*, according to the amount of land held, as may be necessary to make up and provide for such deficit.

14.—Such contributions shall be paid within 21 days of the time the call is made, or the tenancy shall expire and membership cease, as in rule 10.

15.—Clauses 12, 13 shall not apply to buildings or land let therewith, the tenant or tenants of which are not members of the Society, but pay a fixed rent with rates and taxes thereon.

16.—No sub-letting shall be allowed.

17.—A quarter's notice to quit shall be given (in writing) to, or required from each tenant except as in rules 10 and 14, and such notice shall be given by or to the Committee. Such notice to expire at Michaelmas.

18.—Each member shall manure and cultivate his allotment in a husband-like manner, and any member not so manuring and cultivating his allotment, or who, in the opinion of the Committee, shall suffer the allotment to waste to the prejudice of the land, shall be deemed to have infringed the rules of the Society, and the Committee shall give such defaulter due notice to quit.

19.—The members of the Committee, as well as the representatives of the owners of the soil, shall have the right of entry at all times to see the rules of the Society are carried into effect.

20.—No land at present in pasture shall be broken up.

21.—All other land may be used for the cultivation of any corn, grain, roots, herbs, vegetables, flowers, but no standard fruit trees shall be planted or grown thereon unless the consent of the Committee shall have been previously obtained.

22.—No building frames, or pig styes, shall be erected except with the consent of the Committee, and any such building as shall then be erected, shall be erected in such a manner as to be removable at the expiration of the tenancy.

23.—Such erection may be taken to by the incoming tenant at the wish of the outgoing tenant at a valuation to be assessed by the Committee.

24.—Any crop may be taken to by the incoming tenant at the wish of the outgoing tenant at a valuation to be assessed by the Committee.

25.—All questions and disputes between outgoing and incoming tenant, as well as between other members of this Society concerning their holdings from the Society, shall be submitted to the Committee.

26.—A member shall not dig out sand, gravel, or stone on his holding. But when any holding or allotment shall abut upon or be bounded by any hedge, fence, railing, ditch, gutter, watercourse, or accommodation road, then shall the tenant of such holding or allotment be required to keep in repair, trim, clean, scour, and otherwise maintain such hedge, fence, railing, ditch, gutter, watercourse, and accommodation road.

27.—Should any member or members neglect to keep their fences, watercourse, ditches, etc., in proper order, then shall the Committee execute the said repairs and charge the cost to the member or members in default, in proportion or proportions, such proportion or proportions to be repaid at the next quarter day, as if the same were rent, and to be recoverable from the member or members as rent in arrear.

28.—Each member shall be responsible for his boundary posts, and in case of any post or posts being removed, for the expense of re-measuring the allotment as well as replacing the post or posts. He shall further pay a fine of 10s. to the Common Fund should the Committee consider that such removal has been made by himself or any agent of his.

29.—Meetings of the members of the Society shall be held annually within ten days after September 29th, at such time and place as the Committee may decide, and also at such other times and places as the Committee may think necessary.

30.—The chair at all such meetings shall be taken by the Chairman of the Committee, or in his absence a Chairman shall be elected by the meeting.

31.—Each member shall have an equal vote. All questions shall be decided by a majority. No voting by proxy shall be allowed.

32.—No new rule shall be made nor any of the rules herein contained or hereafter to be made shall be amended, altered, or rescinded unless with the consent of a majority of members present at a general meeting of the Society specially called for the purpose. No amendment of rules is valid till registered. No alterations may be made at variance with the leases or terms by which the land is held from its owners.

33.—At the first general meeting held after the Registration of the Society, a Committee of Management shall be elected by a majority of the Members then present ; such Committee to consist of six persons, who may or may not be members of the Society. A Secretary and a Treasurer shall be similarly elected. Members of the Committee as well as others shall be eligible for these offices. Two Auditors who shall not be members of the Society shall be similarly elected. At every annual meeting a Committee of Management, Treasurer, Secretary and two Auditors shall be similarly appointed for the ensuing year, or in failure thereof those last appointed shall be considered as again appointed, and in case any member of the Committee of Management, Treasurer, Secretary or Auditor shall die, resign, or be removed prior to such annual meeting, the Committee of Management shall appoint a person to fill the vacancy. There shall be three Trustees, who may or may not be members of the Committee or of the Society. The Trustees shall continue in office during the pleasure of the Society and be removable at a general meeting, and in case of a vacancy another shall be elected by a majority of members at a meeting called for that purpose. A copy of every resolution appointing a Trustee shall be sent to the Registrar within fourteen days after the date of the meeting at which such resolution was passed in the form prescribed by the Treasury Regulation in that behalf.

34.—Meetings of the Committee shall take place at least four times in each year on or about the usual quarter days, *i.e.*, September 29th, December 25th, March 25th, June 24th, and at such other times and occasions as shall be deemed desirable by any two members of the said Committee, and at least three clear days' notice of such meeting shall be given to each member of the said Committee.

35.—Three members of the Committee of Management duly assembled at any such meeting shall form a quorum, and shall have full power to superintend and conduct the business of this Society according to the rules provided for the government thereof, and shall in all things act for and in the name of this Society, and all acts and orders under the powers delegated to them shall have the like force and effect as the acts and orders of this Society at any general meeting. Every question at such meeting shall be decided by a majority of votes, and if the votes are equal, the Chairman shall have a casting vote. The Committee of Management shall convene all the meetings of the Society, or such requisitions as are herein mentioned.

36.—The Treasurer shall in the month of October in every year, and also when required by a general meeting, or by the Trustees or Committee of Management, upon demand made or notice in writing given to him, or left at his last or usual place of residence, render a just and true account of all moneys received and paid by him on account of the Society, and shall also, on a like demand or notice, pay over all moneys and deliver all property for the time being in his hands or custody to such persons as a general meeting or the Committee of Management or the Trustees appoint. He shall be responsible for such sums of money as may from time to time be paid into his hands by the Secretary or by any person on account of this Society; he shall balance his cash account monthly and supply the Secretary with a duplicate thereof, and shall, if required, attend every general meeting, and he shall have the care of the common seal.

37.—The Secretary shall be present at all meetings of this Society; he shall record correctly the names of the members of the Committee of Management or Trustees there present, and the minutes of their proceedings, which he shall transcribe into a book to be authenticated by the signature of the Chairman as the proceedings of the meeting; he shall receive proposals for admission, and demands for allowances of every description granted by the rules; he shall keep the accounts, documents, and papers of the Society in such manner and for such purposes as the Committee may appoint, and shall prepare and send all returns and other documents required by the Friendly Societies Acts or the Treasury Regulations to be sent to the Registrar. The Secretary shall on all occasions, in the execution of his office, act under the superintendence, control, and directions of the Committee of Management.

38.—The Trustees shall be admitted to all meetings of the Committee of Management, and shall be at liberty to take part in the proceedings thereof, and vote on any question under discussion.

39.—In case any Trustee being removed shall refuse or neglect to assign or transfer any property of the Society as the Committee of Management shall direct, he shall (if he be a member) be expelled the Society, and shall cease to have any claim on the Society on account of any contributions paid by him, without prejudice to any liability to prosecution which he may have incurred.

40.—The Committee shall at its first meeting after the annual Michaelmas meeting elect a Chairman, who may or may not be a member of the Society; such Chairman shall continue in office till another election be made by the Committee.

41.—It shall be the duty of the Committee of Management to provide the Secretary with a sufficient number of copies of the rules, to enable him to deliver to any person on demand a copy of such rules on payment of a sum not exceeding 1s. for non-members, and 6d. for members, and of the Secretary to deliver such copies accordingly.

42. (1.)—The Committee of Management shall cause the accounts of the Society to be regularly entered in proper books.

(2.)—Separate accounts shall be kept of all moneys received or paid on account of every particular fund or benefit assured by the Society, for which a separate table of contributions payable is adopted, distinct from all moneys received and paid on account of any other benefit or fund.

(3.)—A separate account shall also be kept of the expenses of management of the Society and of all contributions on account thereof.

(4.)—The Committee of Management shall once at least in every year submit the accounts, together with a general statement of the same and all necessary vouchers up to the 29th day of September then last, for audit either to one of the public Auditors appointed under the Friendly Societies Act, 1875, or to two or more persons appointed as Auditors by the members at the meeting next before each yearly meeting of the Society, and shall lay before every such meeting a balance sheet (which either may or may not be identical with the annual return, but must not be in contradiction to the same) showing the receipts and expenditure funds and effects of the Society, together with a statement of the affairs of the Society since the last ordinary meeting, and of their then condition. Such Auditors shall have access to all the books and accounts of the Society, and shall examine every balance sheet and annual return of the receipts and expenditure funds and effects of the Society, and shall verify the same with the accounts and vouchers relating thereto, and shall either sign the same as found by them to be correct, duly vouched and in accordance with law, or shall specially report to the meeting of the Society before which the same is laid in what respects they find it incorrect, unvouched, or not in accordance with law.

43. (1.)—Every year before the 1st June, the Committee of Management shall cause the Secretary to send to the Registrar, as required by the Friendly Societies Act, 1875, the annual return in the form prescribed by the Chief Registrar of Friendly Societies, of the receipts and expenditure funds and effects of the Society, and the number of members of the same up to the 29th September then last inclusively, as audited and laid before a general meeting, showing separately the expenditure in respect of the several objects of the Society, together with the copy of the Auditor's report, if any.

(2.)—Such return shall state whether the audit has been conducted by a public Auditor appointed under the Friendly Societies Act, 1875, and by whom, and if such audit has been conducted by any persons other than a public Auditor, shall state the name, address, and calling, or profession of each of such persons, and the manner in which, and the authority under which, they were respectively appointed.

(3.)—It shall be the duty of the Committee of Management to provide the Secretary with a sufficient number of copies of the annual return, or of some balance sheet or other document duly audited containing the same particulars as in the annual return as to the receipts and expenditure funds and effects of the Society, for supplying gratuitously every member or person interested in the funds of the Society, on his application, with a copy of the last annual return of the Society, or of such balance sheet or other document, for the time being, and it shall be the duty of the Secretary to supply such gratuitous copies on application accordingly.

44.—The books and accounts of the Society shall be open to the inspection of any member or person having an interest in the funds of the Society at all reasonable hours at the Registered Office of the Society, or at any place where the same are kept (except that no such member or person, unless he be an officer of the Society, or be specially authorised by a resolution of the Society to do so, shall have the right to inspect the loan or deposit account of any other member without the written consent of such member), and it shall be the duty of the Secretary to produce the same.

(1.)—It shall be the duty of the Committee of Management to keep a copy of the last annual balance sheet of the Society for the time being, together with the report of the Auditors, if any, always hung up in a conspicuous place at the Registered Office of the Society.

45.—So much of the funds of the Society as may not be wanted for immediate use, or to meet the usual accruing liabilities, shall, with the consent of the Committee of Management, or of a majority of the members of the Society present and entitled to vote at a general meeting, be invested by the Trustees in such of the following ways as such Committee or General Meeting shall direct ; namely in any Savings Bank certified under the Act of 1863 of Post Office Savings Bank, in the Public Funds or with the Commissioners for the reduction of the National Debt, or upon Government or real securities in Great Britain or Ireland, or in the purchase of land, or in the erection or alteration of offices or other buildings thereon.

The Committee of Management, with the consent of a Special Meeting of the Society called for the purpose, may purchase or take on lease in names of the Trustees any land, and may sell, exchange, mortgage, lease, or build upon the same (with power to alter and pull down buildings and again rebuild), and no purchaser, assignee, mortgagee, or tenant, shall be bound to inquire as to the authority for any sale, exchange, mortgage or lease by the Trustees, and the receipt of the Trustees shall be a discharge for all moneys arising from or in connection with such sale, exchange, mortgage or lease.

Mortgages or other assurances for securing money to the Society may be vacated by a receipt endorsed, signed by the Trustees, and countersigned by the Secretary in the form contained in the third schedule to the Friendly Societies Act, 1875.

46.—The Society may at any time be dissolved by the consent of three-fourths of the members, testified by their signatures to some instrument of dissolution in the form provided by the Treasury Regulations in that behalf.

47.—If any dispute shall arise between any member or person claiming through a member or under the Rules, and the Society or any officer thereof, it shall be referred to two Arbitrators, one especially chosen by the Committee and one by the person complaining. And the decision of these Arbitrators or of any Umpire they shall call in shall be final and binding.

48.—This Society is subject to the provisions of the Friendly Societies Acts, except so much thereof as relates to annuities (Friendly Societies Act, 1875, sec. 11, subs. 5), appeals from refusal to register a society or any amendment of rules (sec. 11, subs's. 3 and 9, and sec. 13, subs. 3), or from cancelling or suspension of registry (sec. 12, subs. 4 and part of subs. 5), quinquennial valuations (sec. 14, subs. I. f. and part of I. 1, part of subs. 5 and part of schedule 11), certificates of death (sec. 14, subs. 2, sec. 15, subs. 9, and sec. 36 A), exemption from stamp duty (sec. 15, subs. 2), priority on the death, bankruptcy, etc., of officers (sec. 15, subs. 7), loans to members on life assurance (sec. 18, subs. 1), accumulating surplus of contributions for members' use (sec. 19), the amalgamation or transfer of engagements or the dissolution of friendly societies (sec. 24, proviso to subs. 3, and sec. 25, subs. I. c., and subs. 7 and part of schedule II.), militiamen and volunteers (sec. 26), limitations of benefits (sec. 27), payments on the death of children (sec. 28), and societies receiving contributions by collectors (sec. 30).

Rules for a Cow Club.

Below we have the pleasure of reproducing the rules as adopted upon Mr. Edward Heneage's estate :—

1.—That a Cow Club be formed for the parishes of Hainton, South Willingham, Benniworth, Sixhills, Legsby, East Barkwith, and East Torrington, and be called the "Hainton Estate Cow Club."

2.—That the "Hainton Estate Cow Club" do consist of a President, Treasurer, Committee, and other subscription members.

3.—That the Committee consist of three members from each of the parishes of South Willingham and Benniworth, and two each from the parishes of Hainton and Sixhills, in addition to the President and Treasurer, who shall be ex-officio members of the Committee, all of whom (except the President) shall retire at the Annual General Meeting of the Club in April, but be eligible for re-election.

4.—That persons eligible to become members of the Club be tenants on the Hainton estate, paying less than fifty pounds a year rent, or such other cottagers in those parishes as the Committee may consider it desirable to admit.

5.—That the accounts of the Club be balanced on the 31st day of March in each year, and duly audited and examined by the Auditor of the Club (who shall be appointed by the Committee), and presented at the General Meeting.

6.—That a General Meeting of the Club be held on some convenient day (to be fixed by the Committee) within the first fortnight of April.

7.—That each member pay five shillings for each cow entered, and a fee of two shillings and sixpence for every change of cow, and that the subscription be one shilling per month, and paid monthly to the person appointed to receive the same in each district, and shall be paid on the first Monday in each month.

8.—That the Committee shall appoint one of their number in each district to receive members' subscriptions, who shall transmit them before the end of the first whole week in each month to the Treasurer, who shall deposit the same in the Post Office Savings Bank before the last day of the same month.

9.—That any member neglecting to pay his subscriptions for three months in succession shall be warned thereof by the receiver of subscriptions in his district, and if he does not pay up the arrears on the first Monday of the following month, he shall cease to be a member of the Club.

10.—That anyone desirous of entering a cow shall give notice to the members of the Committee in his district, who shall examine into the age, health and value of the cow proposed to be entered.

11.—That no cow be entered in the Club above the age of seven years, nor of the less yearly average value than twelve pounds.

12.—That no member can receive any benefit from the fund whose cow dies of milk fever or lung complaint, if it can be shown that to the owner's knowledge the said cow has had the disease before.

13.—That a marking pincers be provided for the Club for the purpose of marking the cows entered.

14.—That each cow passed by the Committee shall be marked on the ear on the milking side with the Club marker, and no cow shall be deemed duly entered until so marked.

15.—That when any cow is taken ill the owner shall apply to the person who keeps the drinks in his district, who shall go and see the cow, and, if he thinks it necessary, shall direct the owner to call in the farrier without loss of time.

16.—That in case of sudden emergency it shall be in the power of the Committee to allow the owner the cost of any necessary medicine administered, though the Club farrier had not been called in.

17.—That any member of this Society losing a cow be allowed from the fund the sum of twelve pounds.

18.—That no new member receive any benefit from the fund until his cow has been in the Club one month, and the same rule to apply to every additional cow entered.

19.—That no member shall receive any benefit from the Club whose cow exceeds 14 years of age.

20.—That a member losing his cow, and making a claim upon the Club for the same, shall be entitled to the skin, but if anything can be made of the carcase the money arising therefrom shall be paid to the use of the members' fund.

21.—That a Farrier be appointed by the members of the Club, and that a person be appointed in each district to keep a supply of drinks for the use of the Club.

22.—That should any dispute arise as to the interpretation or application of these rules, the same shall be settled by the Committee, whose decision shall be final.

RULES FOR A PIG CLUB.

The following are the rules which regulate the management, etc., of the Pig Club to which nearly all the villagers of —— are proud to belong :—

1.—This Society shall be managed by a Committee of no less than five members and a Secretary.

2.—Any person becoming a member of this Society shall pay one shilling as entrance fee.

3.—That any person wishing to be admitted a benefit member must apply either at the March, June, September, or December Meetings, and shall not be entitled to receive from the Fund until he has been a member six months from the date of his admission.

4.—That every member shall pay sixpence quarterly as contribution money, to be paid in advance.

5.—Any member not paying his subscription every quarter, when due, shall be fined twopence, and if not paid the next quarter night shall be excluded. The quarterly meetings are the first Monday in March, June, September, and December ; the two former months from seven to eight, the latter from eight to nine.

6.—As soon as a member finds his pig unwell he shall inform the Committee, and they shall see it at their earliest convenience, and decide on what course is to be taken ; if thought requisite to kill, and he does not consent, if death ensues the loss shall fall upon himself ; when a dangerous case happens, however, that there is no hope of recovery, he need not acquaint the Committee, but have it killed without delay, and, if not to his advantage to keep it, he may dispose of it.

A Bill always to be produced when a sale is effected, then the loss, if any, to be made up.

7.—If a member is known to ill-treat his pig, or use any unfair means whereby its death is occasioned, he shall not be entitled to any benefit from the fund.

8.—If at any time the fund shall be insufficient to make good a loss, the Committee shall have power to raise an equal levy of all the members.

9.—If a member keep more than one pig, he must insure all, or point out to two or more of the Committee which he will insure.

10.—If a member's pig die in less than a month after he purchased it, he shall receive the same as he gave for it ; if over that period, it shall be valued, and he shall receive according to the value.

11.—If a member purchase a pig, which shall be proved to have been ill at the time he purchased it, and he knew of it, he shall not receive any benefit from the Society.

12.—When the Committee are requested to attend a case, having made an inspection, they are to withdraw from the spot, and privately consider their verdict, and whatever decision they may come to they must inform the member accordingly.

13.—A General Annual Meeting will be held on the first Monday in January, when the Committee and Secretary will be chosen from the members present, to serve the next twelve months ; five of such Committee shall be sufficient to transact business together ; any member of the Committee absenting himself on two successive occasions, when ordered to attend, shall be fined threepence.

14.—Any member obstructing the business of the Society at any meeting thereof shall be fined threepence.

15.—The Committee are particularly requested to show no partiality, but act honestly to all, and endeavour to the best of their judgment to give satisfaction ; they will be required to investigate, strictly, where there is a doubt or suspicion, in order to ascertain how the case stands ; if there is not sufficient proof to convict the member, their decision must be given in his favour.

16.—This Society shall be provided with a box from the funds, to contain the books of account, money, etc. ; the box to be secured by two locks, each lock to differ in its ward ; the keys to be kept by two members of the Committee, who shall be present at the quarterly meetings when the contributions are paid, or send their key, or shall be under a fine of threepence, and the box shall be left in the care of the Secretary.

17.—That if any loss occur not clearly provided for in these rules, the Committee may decide the matter in a fair and just manner between the losing member and the Society.

18.—The Committee to be chosen once a year, as their names stand in the book, or forfeit twopence.

19.—All fines will be strictly enforced.

Secretary...............................

AGREEMENT BETWEEN A LANDLORD AND TENANT FOR AN ALLOTMENT.

Memorandum of Agreement made the ——— day of ——— one thousand eight hundred and ——— between———(hereinafter called " the Landlord ") of the one part, and ——— (hereinafter called " the Tenant ") of the other part.

Whereby the said parties mutually agree as follows :—

The Landlord agrees to let, and the Tenant agrees to take and occupy, for one year from the —— day of ——— next, and so on from year to year, determinable as hereinafter mentioned, ONE GARDEN ALLOTMENT or Piece of Ground, No. —, near to the ——— Road, in the Parish of ———, in the County of ———, being one of the Allotment Gardens there held under the Landlord, at the yearly rent of ———

The said rent to be paid annually on the —— day of ——————, and the first payment of the said rent to become due and be paid on the —— day of ——— next succeeding the date of this Agreement.

The Landlord to pay all rates and taxes chargeable upon the said Allotment.

The Tenant to dig and trench, and also to properly cultivate and manage the said Allotment, and to keep the Land free and clean from weeds.

The Tenant not to assign or underlet the whole or any part of the Allotment without the consent, in writing, of the Landlord.

Either the Landlord or the Tenant may determine this tenancy, at the end of the first or any subsequent year, by giving to the other six calendar months' notice, in writing, ending with the current year ; and, if the Tenant become bankrupt, insolvent, or make any arrangement with his creditors, then the current year's rent shall become immediately payable, and the Landlord shall have power to take immediate possession without any notice.

It shall be lawful for the incoming Tenant of the said Allotment to enter upon it directly the outgoing Tenant has removed his crop, and in no case later than on the ———— day of ———, immediately preceding the termination of the tenancy hereby created, for the purpose of cultivating the same.

If, on the ——— day of —— in any year, an Allotment shall be neglected and in no way prepared for a crop, the Landlord shall have power to take immediate possession of it, without notice, and to re-let it at once.

The Tenant shall at all times co-operate with the Landlord and with the other Allotment-holders in protecting the property of the several Tenants, and in preventing idlers and children from trespassing.

A temporary erection, for the shelter and protection of tools only, is to be permitted on the said Allotment, except with the written consent of the Landlord or his Agent.

As witness the hands of the parties,

(Signature)... ....

D

AGREEMENT TO LET A COW TO A LABOURER, ETC.

The following is a copy of an agreement which has been used with great success :—

Agreement between _____ _____ of _____ ————, hereinafter called "the owner," of the one part, and ——— of —— hereinafter called "the hirer," of the other part : Whereby the said owner agrees to let, and the said hirer agrees to hire, from the 1st day of May, 189—, from year to year, a three years' old Irish heifer, No. 150, coloured red and white, weighing 50 imperial stones, value £10 (being four shillings per stone), the property of the said owner, at the yearly hire, and subject to the conditions hereinafter mentioned, that is to say :

1.—The hirer shall pay to Mr. ————, of ————, or other agent for the time being of the owner, for the use and produce of the cow (No. 150) the clear annual sum of two pounds and ten shillings, being equal to one shilling per imperial stone of the live weight of the heifer on the 1st of May, 188—.

2.—The cow shall at all times be properly fed and carefully attended to by the hirer, who shall provide pasture for summer, and not less than 250 imperial stones (being five times the cow's weight) of good hay for its winter maintenance ; and in addition to hay and grass, the hirer shall provide 50 imperial stones (the cow's weight) of cake, meal, and bran, to be given during the year.

3.—The cow to be sent to a yearling bull the second time it comes in service after calving, and to be "dried" six weeks before it is due to calve, and whilst dry to be allowed 2 lbs. per day of linseed cake in addition to hay or grass.

4.—In case of illness or accident, immediate notice thereof shall be given by the hirer to the owner, or his agent, and the hirer shall, if necessary, promptly employ an experienced farrier, half of whose charges shall be borne by the owner, and half by the hirer ; and should the illness be pleuro-pneumonia, or any other contagious disease, the hirer shall give immediate notice to the Government inspector for the district.

5.—In the event of permanent injury to, or death of, the cow from illness or accident, the loss shall be borne by the owner ; but the hirer shall not be entitled to any compensation whatsoever from the owner, or to any allowance, except as provided for in the fourth condition.

6.—The hirer shall have the right, on giving three months' notice, to purchase the cow at the end of the first or any year for £10, being the price at which it was valued on the 1st of May, 189—, as named above.

7.—This agreement may be terminated on the 30th day of April in any year, either upon the owner giving to the hirer, or the hirer giving to the owner, or his agent, three months' previous notice in writing ; and on the expiration of such notice the cow shall be returned to the owner at the hirer's expense, provided always that, in the event of the cow being due to calve before the expiration of such notice, the cow shall be returned to the owner one week before it is due to calve.

8.—The hirer may return the cow to the owner at any time during the year without notice, provided it is fat enough for beef, and if it realises more than its value when hired, he shall receive any additional price that it makes.

9.—If and whenever the hirer shall be adjudged a bankrupt, or commit any act of bankruptcy, or if his affairs shall be liquidated by arrangement or composition, or if he shall make any assignment for the benefit of creditors, the owner may resume or take possession of the cow, wherever the same may be, without making any compensation whatsoever, and may plead the leave and license of the hires for any trespass committed or complained of in resuming or retaking such possession.

(Signed) _____(Owner).

(Signed) _____(Hirer).

Dated this 1st day of May, 189—.

Witness.

We understand that the system of hiring out cows has been adopted by the owner, who uses the above Agreement, for some twelve or thirteen years, and has been in every sense a success, the cows paying a profit both to the persons who hire and to the person who lets them. It seems that the capital invested has yielded during the first five years 5 per cent. per annum, and afterwards no less than from 7½ to 10 per cent. The hirer, it is argued, should have the privilege of purchasing the cow at the end of the year, at the price it was valued when hired out, an arrangement which is liberal and conceived in a large-hearted spirit. A good dairy heifer increases considerably by the time she has her second calf, and the hirer, therefore, who has this privilege, can secure a cow for say £9 or £10, which at the time he actually buys her is really worth £11 or £12. He has, too, the opportunity of buying an animal whose value as a milk producer and butter maker is well known.

In addition to the various agreements, etc., named, we give below a copy of the " Model " Regulations, Application, and Agreement issued by the Local Government Board in 1888. These were issued in connection with the Allotments Act, 1887 (section 6). Under the Local Government Act, 1894 (section 9, sub-section 14), they are applicable to Parish Councils, and wherever the words "Sanitary Authority" are employed, they may be altered to " Parish Council."

REGULATIONS.

Made by the [1]——————————————————————as the [2]————— Sanitary Authority for the District of[3]——————————with respect to allotments for the [4]——————————.

Interpretation of terms.—1. Throughout these Regulations the expression " the Sanitary Authority " means the [1]——————————as the [2]—————————Sanitary Authority, or, if and so long as there are Allotment Managers who are empowered to carry out these Regulations, such Managers ; the expression " the District " means the [3]————— Sanitary District of[4]——————————and the expression " the Parish " means [5]——————————.

For defining the persons eligible to be tenants of the Allotments.—2. Any man or woman, of not less than twenty-one years of age, who at the time of application to the Sanitary Authority for an allotment has been resident in the [6]——————————for not less than————————months, and belongs to the labouring population, shall be eligible to become a tenant of an allotment.

Provided always that a person who, at the time of such application, already holds an allotment, either from the Sanitary Authority or other-

---

[1] " Mayor, Aldermen, and Burgesses of the Borough of——.——, " acting by the Council "; *or*, " Improvement Commissioners for the " District of——————, acting "; *or*, " Local Board for the District " of——————, acting "; *or*, " Guardians of the Poor of the—————— " Union, acting," *as the case may be.*

[2] *Insert* " urban " *or* " rural."

[3] *Insert the name of the district.*

[4] *Insert* " said district " *or* " parish of——————— " *as the case may be.*

[5] *If, in a rural Sanitary District, the allotments are provided for a contributory place which is not co-extensive with a poor law parish, the area should be described by the name of the contributory place.*

[6] *Insert* " district " *or* " parish."

wise, shall not be eligible to become tenant of an allotment, the area of which, together with the area of any allotment or allotments already held by him, would amount to more than———————.

As to dividing the land into Allotments.—3. The Sanitary Authority, before giving notice of their intention to let any allotment, shall divide the land, and shall cause a plan to be prepared, showing each allotment, and distinguishing it by a separate number. They shall enter each allotment under its number in the register required to be kept, showing the particulars of the tenancy, acreage, and rent of every allotment.

The Sanitary Authority may from time to time re-divide any portion of the land. They shall enter and number each allotment formed on such re-division in the register, in the manner hereinbefore prescribed.

For defining the notices to be given for the letting of the Allotments. —4. The Sanitary Authority shall give public notice, by bills or placards posted in some conspicuous places in the [1]——————, or otherwise exhibited therein, setting forth the particulars as to any allotments which they propose to let.

Such notice shall specify the allotments to be let and the size thereof, the rent to be paid for the same, the place to which, and the name of the person to whom application for the hiring of any allotment is to be sent, and the last day for receiving any such application.

For defining the size of the Allotments.—5. The size of any allotment let by the Sanitary Authority shall not be less than [2]———poles.

For regulating the letting of the Allotments and preventing any undue preference in the letting thereof.—6. The Sanitary Authority shall not let any allotment unless and until notice that they propose to let the same has been duly given in pursuance of the Regulation in that behalf at least [3]———weeks before the last day for receiving applications to hire such allotment.

Every person who shall apply for an allotment shall furnish in the form hereto appended a true statement of the particulars therein required to be specified, and shall send or deliver the same to the clerk to the [4]——————————————, and it shall be the duty of such clerk to number the applications in the order in which they are received.

In letting an allotment for which there are two or more applicants eligible to become tenants, the Sanitary Authority shall select the applicant who appears most likely to keep the allotment in a proper state of cultivation; but in cases of equality in this respect the Sanitary Authority shall give preference to the applicants according to the order in which their applications are numbered as having been received.

---

[1] *Insert* "district" *or* "parish."

[2] *It is suggested that* "twenty" *should be inserted here.*

[3] "Two" *might be inserted.*

[4] *Insert the name of the Urban or Rural Sanitary Authority of the District.*

FORM OF APPLICATION FOR ALLOTMENTS.

To the————————Sanitary Authority for the District of————
————————————————————, *or*, To the
Allotment Managers for the————————————of————
I, the undersigned, hereby make application for No.————of the
allotments provided for the District [*or* Parish of————————].

1. Name————————————————————
2. Residence————————————————
3. Age————————
4. Occupation————————————— -
5. How long resident in the District [*or* Parish]——————————
6. Whether holding any Allotment, and if so—
    (*a*) From whom——————————————
    (*b*) Extent of Allotment—————————————
              Signature————————————————
              Date————————————————————

7. When the Sanitary Authority have decided to let any allotment or allotments to any person, an agreement shall be made between the Sanitary Authority and such person, and shall be signed by the clerk to the [1] ————————————————————— on behalf of the Sanitary Authority and by such person. The agreement shall be in the form hereinafter prescribed, or to the like effect.

FORM OF AGREEMENT FOR LETTING.

Agreement made this————day of————18-—, between the ——————————————————————(hereinafter called the Sanitary Authority) of the one part, and———————— of————————————(hereinafter called the tenant) of the other part, whereby the said Sanitary Authority agree to let, and the said tenant agrees to hire the allotment [*or* allotments] numbered ————————————in the register of allotments provided for the District [*or* Parish of————————], and containing———————— or thereabouts, at the yearly rent of———————— , and at a proportionate rent for any period of less than a year over which the tenancy may extend, subject to the following conditions :—

(*a*) The rent shall be paid [2] ——————————————————on the ——————————————day of——————————, the ——————————————day of——————————, the ——————————————day of——————— and the ———————— day of——————— in each year.

---

[1] *Insert the name of the Urban or Rural Sanitary Authority of the District.*
[2] *Insert* " in advance," *if this is intended.*

(*b*) Any member or officer of the Sanitary Authority shall be entitled at any time when directed by the Sanitary Authority to enter and inspect the allotment.

(*c*) The tenancy, if not sooner terminated by the Sanitary Authority in pursuance of the Allotments Act, 1887, or of any Regulations made thereunder, shall terminate on the death of the tenant, or after————months' notice in writing given by the tenant, such notice to expire on the————————or————————.

Signed —————————————

Clerk to the—————————

Witness——————————

Signed —————————————

Tenant————————————

Witness———————————

For defining the conditions under which the Allotments are to be cultivated.—8. Every person to whom an allotment may have been let shall cultivate such allotment according to the following conditions, that is to say :

He shall keep the allotment free from weeds, and well manured, and otherwise maintain it in a proper state of cultivation ;

He shall not plant any trees or shrubs so as to be injurious to any adjacent allotment ;

He shall keep every hedge that shall form part of the allotment properly cut and trimmed ;

He shall not cause any nuisance or annoyance to the tenant of any other allotment.

As to the reasonable notice to be given to a tenant of any Allotment of the determination of his tenancy.—9. The Sanitary Authority shall give to the tenant of any allotment not less than————————months' notice of the determination of his tenancy, such notice to take effect on————————————or ——————————————

Provided always that this regulation shall not apply in the case of the determination of a tenancy in pursuance of the statutory provision in that behalf, where the rent is in arrear for not less than forty days, or where it appears to the Sanitary Authority that the tenant of an allotment, not less than three months after the commencement of the tenancy thereof, has not duly observed the regulations affecting such allotment, or is resident more than one mile out of the [1]————————.

For prescribing the manner in which the Register of Allotments shall be open to the examination of ratepayers.—10. The register showing the particulars of the tenancy, acreage, and rent of every allotment let, and of the unlet allotments, shall be deposited at the office of the———————————, and shall be open during office hours to the examination of any ratepayer in the [1]————————.

————————

[1] *Insert* " district " *or* " parish."

PART II.—SMALL HOLDINGS.

CHAPTER VI.

LEGISLATION.

CONCURRENTLY with the agitation which resulted in the enactment of the Allotment Acts, 1887 and 1890, was an agitation for small holdings—*i.e.*, holdings of land larger in extent than allotments, to the cultivation of which a man could devote his whole energies, and which held out to him a career upon the land for the continuance of his previous successful effort, ability, and thrift. As a result the Small Holdings Act, 1892, was passed into law, and we desire to see it gradually and extensively put into operation. The Act has met with the approval of legislators; and, in theory, is meeting with more and more approval by land-owners, on whom it chiefly rests to make the measure successful or the reverse, seeing that it contains no compulsory clauses. We say theory advisedly, as we shall presently show.

We wish first, however, to give an exact copy of this measure—a measure which is as novel as it may be useful and important.

THE SMALL HOLDINGS ACT, 1892.

PART I.—PROVISION OF SMALL HOLDINGS BY COUNTY COUNCILS.

1.—(1) If the Council of any County are of opinion that there is such a demand for small holdings in their County as justifies them in putting into operation this Part of this Act, the Council may, subject to the provisions of this Act, acquire any suitable land for the purpose of providing small holdings for persons whq desire to buy and will themselves cultivate the holdings. (2) The expression "small holding" for the purposes of this Act shall mean land acquired by a Council under the powers and for the purposes of this Act, and which exceeds one acre and either does not exceed fifty acres, or, if exceeding fifty acres, is o₁ an annual value for the purposes of the income tax not exceeding fifty pounds.

2.—Where land through its proximity to a town, or suitability for building purposes, or for any other special reason, has a prospective value which in the opinion of the County Council is too high to make its purchase for agricultural purposes desirable, the Council may hire the land on lease or otherwise for the purpose of letting it in small holdings in accordance with the provisions of this Act.

3.—(1) For the purpose of the purchase of land under this Act by a County Council, the Lands Clauses Acts shall be incorporated with this Act, except the provisions of those Acts with respect to the purchase and taking of land otherwise than by agreement, which provisions shall not apply for the purposes of this Act ; and section one hundred and seventy-eight of the Public Health Act, 1875, shall apply as if the County Council were referred to therein. (2) The County Council may, if they think fit, before sale or letting, adapt for small holdings any land acquired under this Act by dividing and fencing it, making occupation roads, and executing any other works, such as works for the provision of drainage or water supply, which can in the opinion of the Council be more economically and efficiently executed for the land as a whole. (3) The County Council may also, if they think fit, as part of the agreement for the sale or letting of a small holding, adapt the land for a small holding by erecting thereon such buildings, or making such adaptations of existing buildings, as in their opinion are required for the due occupation of the holding, and cannot be made by the purchaser or tenant.

4.—(1) The County Council shall apportion the total cost of the acquisition of the land, and of any adaptation thereof, among the several holdings in such manner as seems just, and shall, save as hereinafter mentioned, offer the small holdings for sale in accordance with rules under this Act. (2) Where the County Council are of opinion that any persons desirous of themselves cultivating small holdings are unable to buy, on the terms fixed by this Act, or where the land has been hired by the Council on lease or otherwise, the Council may, in the case of any small holding which either does not exceed fifteen acres in extent, or if exceeding fifteen acres is of the annual value for the purpose of the income tax not exceeding fifteen pounds, instead of offering it for sale, offer to let it in accordance with rules under this Act. Provided that a tenant of any small holding may, before the expiration of his tenancy, remove any fruit and other trees and bushes planted or acquired by him for which he has no claim for compensation, and remove any tool-house, shed, green-house, fowl-house, or pig-sty built or acquired by him for which he has no claim for compensation.   (3) The County Council shall have power to sell, or, in the case of small holdings which may be let, to let one or more small holdings to a number of persons working on a co-operative system, provided such system be approved by the County Council.   (4) The cost of acquisition and adaptation shall for the purposes of this section include every expense incurred by the Council in relation to the land, inclusive of any allowance to any officers of the Council for work done in relation thereto.

5.—(1) Any County Council may, and every County Council not being a Council of a county borough shall, appoint a committee to consider whether the circumstances of the county justify the Council in putting into operation this Part of this Act.   (2) Any one or more county electors may present a petition to the Council of their county alleging that there is a demand for small holdings in the county, and praying that this Part of this Act may be put in operation, and thereupon the petition shall be referred to the committee appointed under this section, who, on being satisfied that the petition is presented in good faith and on reasonable grounds, shall forthwith cause an inquiry into the circumstances to be made, and shall report the result to the Council.   (3) If any councillor representing or alderman residing in any electoral division of a county in which it is alleged that there is a demand for small holdings is not a member of the committee, he shall be added to the committee for the consideration of the alleged demand.

6.—(1) The purchase money for each small holding sold by the County Council shall include the costs of registration of title, but shall not include any expense incurred by the purchaser for legal or other advice or assistance.   (2) Every purchaser shall, within such time, not less than one month after the purchase, as is fixed by rules under this Act, complete the purchase.   (3) On such completion he shall pay not less than one fifth of the purchase money.   (4) A portion representing not more than one fourth of the purchase money may, if the County Council think fit, be secured by a perpetual rentcharge, which shall be redeemable in manner directed by section forty-five of the Conveyancing and Law of Property Act, 1881, with respect to rentcharges to which that section applies.   (5) The residue (if any) of the purchase money shall be secured by a charge on the holding in favour of the Council, and shall either be repaid by half-yearly instalments of principal with such interest, and within such term not exceeding fifty years from the date of the sale, as may be agreed on with the Council, or shall, if the purchaser so requires, be repaid with such interest and within such term as aforesaid by a terminable annuity payable by equal half-yearly instalments.   The amount for the time being unpaid may at any time be discharged, and any such terminable annuity may at any time be redeemed, in accordance with tables fixed by the County Council. (6) The Council may, if they think fit, agree to postpone for a term not exceeding five years the time for payment of all or any part of an instalment either of principal or interest or of a terminable annuity, in consideration of expenditure by the purchaser which, in the opinion of the Council, increases the value of the holding, but shall do so on such terms as will, in their opinion, prevent them from incurring any loss. (7) A small holding may be sold subject to such rights of way or other rights for the benefit of other small holdings as the Council consider necessary or expedient.

7.—Every County Council acquiring land under this Act shall make rules[1] for carrying into effect this Act, except as otherwise provided, and in particular—(*a*) as to the manner in which holdings are to be sold or let or offered for sale or letting ; and (*b*) as to the notice to be given of the offer for sale or letting ; and (*c*) for guarding against any small holding being let or sold to a person who is unable to cultivate it properly, and otherwise for securing the proper cultivation of a holding.

8.—Every County Council shall keep a list of the owners and occupiers of small holdings sold or let by them, and a map or plan showing the size, boundaries, and situation of each small holding so sold or let.

9.—(1) Every small holding sold by a County Council under this Act shall for a term of twenty years from the date of the sale, and thereafter so long as any part of the purchase money remains unpaid, be held subject to the following conditions :—(*a*) That any periodical payments due in respect of the purchase money shall be duly made ; (*b*) That the holding shall not be divided, subdivided, assigned, let, or sublet without the consent of the County Council ; (*c*) That the holding shall be cultivated by the owner or occupier as the case may be, and shall not be used for any purpose other than agriculture ; (*d*) That not more than one dwelling-house shall be erected on the holding ; (*e*) That any dwelling-house erected on the holding shall comply with such requirements as the County Council may impose for securing healthiness and freedom from overcrowding ; (*f*) That no dwelling-house or building on the holding shall be used for the sale of intoxicating liquors ; (*g*) In the case of any holding on which, in the opinion of the County Council, a dwelling-house ought not to be erected, that no dwelling-house shall be erected on the holding without the consent of the County Council. (2) If any such condition is broken, the Council may, after giving the owner an opportunity of remedying the breach, if it is capable of remedy, cause the holding to be sold. (3) If on the decease of the owner while the holding is subject to the conditions imposed by this section, the holding would, by reason of any devise, bequest, intestacy, or otherwise, become subdivided, the Council may require the holding to be sold within twelve months after such decease to some one person, and if default is made in so selling the holding, the Council may cause the holding to be sold. (4) Any sale by the County Council under this section may be made either subject to the charge in respect of purchase money, or free, wholly or partly, from that charge, and in either case the provisions of this Act with respect to the purchase money shall apply in like

---

[1] See Appendix B.

manner as if the sale were the first sale of a small holding under this Act. (5) The proceeds of the sale shall be applied in discharge of any unpaid purchase money for the holding or redemption of any rentcharge or terminable annuity which is not to continue a charge on the holding, and, subject as aforesaid, shall be paid to the person appearing to the Council to be entitled to receive the same. (6) The County Council may, under special circumstances, to be recorded in their minutes, sell or consent to the sale under this section of a small holding free from all or any of the conditions imposed by this section, and may give such consent on such terms as they think fit. (7) Every small holding let by a County Council under the foregoing provisions of this Act shall be held subject to the conditions on which it would under this section be held if it were sold, except so far as those conditions relate to the purchase money ; and, if any such condition or any term of the letting is broken, the Council may, after giving the tenant an opportunity of remedying the breach (if it is capable of remedy), determine the tenancy. (8) Nothing in or done under this section shall derogate from the effect of any building or sanitary byelaws for the time being in force.

10.—(1) When a County Council have purchased land under this Act, they shall apply for their registration as proprietors thereof with an absolute title under the Land Transfer Act, 1875. (2) Rules[1] under the Land Transfer Act, 1875, may – (a) adapt that Act to the registration of small holdings, with such modifications as appear to be required ; and (b) on the application and at the expense of a County Council provide, by the appointment of local agents or otherwise, for carrying into effect the objects of this section.

11.—If at any time after the restrictive conditions imposed by this Act have ceased to attach to a small holding, the owner of the holding desires to use the holding for purposes other than agriculture, he shall, before so doing, whether the holding is situate within a town or built upon or not, offer the holding for sale, first to the County Council from whom the holding was purchased, next to the person or persons (if any) then entitled to the lands from which the holding was originally severed, and then to the person or persons whose lands immediately adjoin the holding, and sections one hundred and twenty-seven to one hundred and thirty of the Lands Clauses Consolidation Act, 1845, shall apply as if the owner of the small holding were the promoter of the undertaking, and the holding were superfluous lands within the meaning of those sections.

12.—Where a person having the powers of a tenant for life within the meaning of the Settled Land Act, 1882, sells, exchanges, or leases, any settled land to a County Council for the purposes of this Act, such sale, exchange, or lease may be made at such a price, or for such consideration, or at such rent as, having regard to the said purposes and to all the circumstances of the case, is the best that can be reasonably obtained.

[1] See Appendix C.

13.--A person having the powers of a tenant for life within the meaning of the Settled Land Act, 1882, may grant the settled land, or a part thereof, to a County Council for the purposes of this Act in perpetuity, at a fee farm or other rent secured by condition of re-entry, or otherwise as may be agreed upon.

14 —Where any right of grazing, sheep-walk, or other similar right is attached to land acquired by a County Council for the purposes of small holdings, the Council may attach any share of the right to any small holding in such manner and subject to such regulations as they think expedient.

15.—(1) A County Council shall, if practicable, sell or let as small holdings, and in accordance with this Act, any land acquired under this Act, but if the Council are of opinion that any such land is not needed for, or is unsuitable for, small holdings, or cannot be sold or let under the foregoing provisions of this Act, or that some more suitable land is available, they may sell or let the land otherwise than under the said provisions, or exchange the land for other land more suitable for small holdings, and may pay or receive money for equality of exchange, and may erect such buildings or execute such other works as will in the opinion of the Council enable the land to be sold or let without loss ; (2) The Council may also, while any sale of a holding is pending in pursuance of this Act, temporarily let or manage the holding for such time and in such manner as they think expedient ; (3) Sections one hundred and twenty-eight to one hundred and thirty-two of the Lands Clauses Consolidation Act, 1845 (relating to the right of pre-emption of superfluous lands) shall apply upon any sale in pursuance of this section before any such buildings or works as aforesaid are erected or executed on the land proposed to be sold, but save as aforesaid the provisions of the Lands Clauses Consolidation Act, 1845, with respect to the sale of superfluous lands, shall not apply.

16.—(1) Where a County Council provide small holdings they may delegate, with or without restrictions, the powers of the County Council under this Act with respect to the adaptation of land for any holdings, and the sale, letting, and management of any holdings to a Committee consisting of—The County Councillor representing the electoral division in which the holdings are situate ; and two other members of the County Council ; and two of the allotment managers (if any) under the Allotments Act, 1887, for the parish or area in which the holdings are situate selected by those managers, or if there are no allotment managers, two persons appointed in manner provided by that Act for the appointment of allotment managers ; or if the holdings are situate within the limits of a municipal borough, then, instead of the persons selected or appointed as aforesaid, two members of the Borough Council ; and in the construction of this Act references to the County Council shall, in their application to the powers so delegated, include any such Committee. Provided that a County Council shall not under this section delegate any powers of making or levying a rate or of borrowing money ; (2) The Local Government Act, 1888, shall apply to any Committee appointed under this section as if it were appointed under that Act.

PART II.—LOANS BY COUNTY COUNCILS TO TENANTS PURCHASING
SMALL HOLDINGS.

17.—(1) Where the tenant of a small holding has agreed with his landlord for the purchase of the holding, the County Council of the County in which the holding or any part of it is situate may, if they think fit, advance to the tenant on the security of the holding an amount not exceeding four-fifths of the purchase money thereof; (2) The provisions of this Act with respect to the purchase money secured by a charge on a small holding sold by a County Council, and with respect to any small holding so sold, shall apply to an advance made and a holding purchased under this section, as if the advance was the purchase money, save that the County Council shall not guarantee the title of the purchaser of the holding; (3) No advance shall be made by a County Council under this section, unless they are satisfied that the title to the holding is good, that the sale is made in good faith, and that the price is reasonable.

PART III.—SUPPLEMENTAL.

18.—(1) A County Council shall not acquire land under this Act save at such price that, in the opinion of the Council, all expenses incurred by the Council in relation to the land will be recouped out of the purchase money for the land sold by the Council, or in the case of land let, out of the rent, and shall fix the purchase money or rent at such reasonable amount as will, in their opinion, guard them against loss; (2) A County Council shall not take any proceedings under this Act whereby the charge for the time being on the county rate, for the purposes of this Act, including the annual payments in respect of the loans raised for those purposes, is, in the opinion of the Council, likely to exceed in any one year the amount produced by a rate of a penny in the pound, and, where the said charge at any time is equal or nearly equal to that amount, no further land shall be purchased in pursuance of this Act, until the charge has been decreased so as to admit of the further purchase without the charge exceeding the said amount.

19.—(1) A County Council may borrow money for the purposes of this Act in accordance with the Local Government Act, 1888, or, if the Council of a county borough, with the Public Health Act, 1875, except that any money so borrowed shall, notwithstanding anything in either of those Acts, be repaid within such period not exceeding fifty years, as the Council, with the consent of the Local Government Board, determine in each case. Provided that money borrowed under this Act shall not be reckoned as part of the total debt of a county for the purpose of section sixty-nine, sub-section two, of the Local Government Act, 1888; (2) The Public Works Loan Commissioners may, in manner provided by the Public Works Loans Act, 1875, lend any money which may be borrowed by a County Council for the purposes of this Act;

(3) Every loan by the Public Works Loan Commissioners in pursuance of this Act shall bear such rate of interest not less than three pounds two shillings and sixpence per cent. per annum, as the Treasury may authorise as being in their opinion sufficient to enable such loans to be made without loss to the Exchequer ; (4) Any capital money received by a County Council in payment or discharge of purchase money for land sold by them, or in repayment of an advance made by them, shall be applied, with the sanction of the Local Government Board, either in repayment of debt or for any other purpose for which capital money may be applied ; (5) The expenses incurred by the Council of a county borough under this Act shall be defrayed out of the borough fund or borough rate, and any money borrowed by such a Council shall be borrowed on the security of the borough fund or borough rate.

20.—For the purposes of this Act—The expressions "agriculture" and "cultivation" shall include horticulture and the use of land for any purpose of husbandry, inclusive of the keeping or breeding of live stock, poultry or bees, and the growth of fruit, vegetables, and the like : the expression "county" shall mean the area under the authority of a County Council : the expression "County Council" shall include the Council of a county borough, and the expression "electoral division" in its application to a county borough divided into wards shall mean ward, and in its application to a county borough the expression "county rate" shall mean the borough rate or borough fund : the expression "county elector" shall include "burgess." In this Act, and in the enactments incorporated with this Act, the expression "land" shall include any right or easement in or over land.

21.—In the application of this Act to Scotland—(1) A reference to any sections of the Lands Clauses Consolidation Act, 1845, shall be construed as a reference to the corresponding sections of the Lands Clauses Consolidation (Scotland) Act, 1845 ; (2) A reference to the Local Government Act, 1888, shall be construed as a reference to the Local Government (Scotland) Act, 1889 ; (3) The Secretary for Scotland shall be substituted for the Local Government Board ; (4) The expression "county rate" shall mean the general purposes rate leviable by a County Council ; (5) The expression "devise" shall mean *mortis causa* disposition : (6) The expression "easement" shall mean servitude ; (7) The references to county boroughs shall not apply ; (8) The expression "county elector" shall have the same meaning as in the Local Government (Scotland) Act, 1889.

22.—With respect to the unpaid purchase money for a small holding under this Act, the following provisions shall have effect in Scotland in lieu of sub-sections four and five of section six of this Act :—(1) A portion, representing not more than one-fourth of the purchase money, may, if the County Council think fit, be converted into a perpetual rentcharge which shall be a real burden affecting the holding, redeemable at any time at the option of the purchaser in accordance with tables fixed by the County Council, and the certificate of the county clerk that the redemption money has been paid shall, without any other instrument, operate as an extinction of the rentcharge, and the registration of such certificate in the register of sasines shall be equivalent to the registration of a discharge of the said rentcharge : (2) The residue (if any) of the purchase money shall be secured by a bond which shall be a charge on the holding in favour of the County Council, and shall either be repaid by half-yearly instalments of principal with such interest and within such term not exceeding fifty years from the date of the sale as may be agreed on with the Council, or shall, if the purchaser so requires, be repaid with such interest and within such term by a terminable annuity payable by half-yearly instalments. The amount for the time being unpaid may at any time be discharged, and any such terminable annuity may at any time be redeemed in accordance with tables fixed by the County Council. A certificate by the county clerk that the whole of the said residue has been paid, or that such terminable annuity has been redeemed, shall, without any other instrument, operate as a discharge of the said residue and extinction of the said terminable annuity, as the case may be, and the registration of such certificate in the register of sasines shall be equivalent to the registration of a discharge of the said bond.

23.—In Scotland the County Council shall cause to be prepared and duly registered all deeds, writs, and instruments, necessary for completing the title of the purchaser of a small holding, and for securing the payment of any unpaid purchase money, and shall include in the purchase money the cost so incurred, or to be incurred, according to scales set forth in tables fixed by the County Council. Provided that— (1) the County Council, if they think fit, may appoint a person duly qualified (in the opinion of the sheriff) to carry out the provisions of this section, and shall assign to him such salary or other remuneration as they may determine ; and (2) the County Council shall not be liable for any expenses incurred by the purchaser of a small holding for legal or other advice or assistance rendered to him on his own employment. Sections 10, 12, and 13 of this Act shall not apply to Scotland.

24.—A Committee of a County Council appointed under this Act with respect to the adaptation of land for small holdings, and the sale, letting, and management of the holdings, shall, in Scotland, consist of—the County Councillor representing the electoral division in which the holdings are situate ; and two other members of the County Council ; and two persons elected triennially by the county electors in the electoral division aforesaid, in accordance with such regulations as the Secretary for Scotland may from time to time prescribe, whether preliminary or incidental to such election, and for applying to such election any enactments as to offences at the election of County Councillors, and for supplying casual vacancies on the Committee ; or if the holdings are situate within the limits of any burgh, then, instead of the persons elected as aforesaid, two town councillors or commissioners, as the case may be, to be appointed for that purpose by the Town Council or commissioners of such burgh.

25.—This Act shall not apply to Ireland.

26.—This Act shall come into operation on the first day of October, one thousand eight hundred and ninety-two.

27.—This Act may be cited as the Small Holdings Act, 1892.

It is obvious that the object of the Act is to create a race of small cultivating owners, and thus to procure a wider distribution of land among the people of the country. We may, perhaps, give a *resumé* of the leading features :— A " small holding " means a portion of land exceeding one acre and not exceeding fifty acres in extent, or, if exceeding fifty acres, not exceeding £50 annual value. Any one or more county electors may present a petition to the County Council of their own county, stating that there is a demand for small holdings in the county. This petition is then to be referred to a committee of the Council of which the local councillor is a member, and if the committee are satisfied that the petition is presented in good faith and on reasonable grounds they must forthwith hold a local inquiry. If the Council are then satisfied that the demand is genuine, it is their duty to acquire, if possible, suitable land for the purpose of providing small holdings for persons who desire them and who will themselves cultivate them. Every man who purchases a small holding will be required to pay down one-fifth of the purchase-money, and the balance in half-yearly payments during a term of not more than fifty years. If the council think fit, a portion not exceeding one-fourth of the purchase-money may remain unpaid, and be secured by a perpetual rent-charge upon the holding. This may, perhaps, be better understood by a simple illustration :—Supposing a man wishes to purchase a small holding, the total cost of which is £100. He will first have to pay down a sum of £20. Then on the £80 still remaining he would pay a small half-yearly sum, so as, within a period not exceeding fifty years, to pay off the principal (that is to say, the £80) and the interest thereon. If the County Council borrow the money at 3 or $3\frac{1}{8}$ per cent., as they probably will be able to do, and charge the small holder 1 per cent. additional to provide

E

what is called a "sinking fund," the half-yearly payment would only be £1 13s. Whilst the object of the Act is to create a class of small *cultivating owners* of land, advantages are also offered to those who cannot pay down the fifth of the purchase-money, or who may require their capital for purchasing stock, etc. To such persons the County Council have power to let small holdings, either up to fifteen acres each, or, if exceeding fifteen acres, then up to £15 annual value. Another important clause gives the County Council power to let or sell small holdings to a number of persons working on a co-operative system, the rules first being approved by the Council. There is also provision in the Act for loans to sitting tenants who wish to purchase their present holdings from their landlords. The County Council have the power to advance four-fifths of the purchase-money, which can be paid off as in the case of those holdings purchased direct from the County Council. Every small holding must be cultivated by the owner or tenant, and must not be used for any purpose other than agriculture. Nor can it be sublet. A dwelling-house may be erected on the holding, but no such house can be used for the sale of intoxicating liquor. If the purchaser of a small holding makes permanent improvements to his holding, the Council may postpone the payments due from him for any period not exceeding five years. Where any right of grazing, sheep-walk, or other similar right is attached to land acquired by the County Council for small holdings, the County Council have the power to continue a share of such right to any small holding they may sell or hire.

Those would-be small holders desiring to take advantage of the Act, having first agreed with the local landowner or landowners for the purchase from them of the land, may then petition the County Council to put the enactment into operation. To assist them to do this we have drawn up a petition suitable for the purpose.

PETITION TO COUNTY COUNCIL BY COUNTY ELECTORS DESIRING SMALL HOLDINGS.

THE SMALL HOLDINGS ACT, 1892.

(Section 5, subsection 2.)

To the ——— County Council.

GENTLEMEN,

We, the undersigned, county electors, hereby beg to state that there is such a demand for small holdings in the county as is contemplated under the Small Holdings Act, 1892 ; and we respectfully pray that the Act may be put into operation on our behalf by the Council with the view of satisfying the said demand.

Names of County Electors.	Full Address.

In the letter sent to the Clerk to the Council accompanying the above petition, it would be convenient to the Council, and save time to all concerned, if the quantity of land desired, place, exact situation, names and addresses of owners, and of present tenants (if any), etc., were stated. It is, be it noted, not absolutely necessary that the petition to the Council should be made by those who *want* the land. County electors *not* desiring small holdings may make a petition on behalf of those who do ; in which case the words "on our behalf" should be left out ; but in forwarding the petition to the Council, the person or persons doing so should state, in addition to the particulars already suggested, the names and addresses of the parties actually wanting the ground.

In concluding this chapter we would mention that the Small Holdings Act, passed as a "Government" measure, is based on Mr. Jesse Collings' Bill, containing, as it does, proposals identical with those embodied in the second and third parts of the three-fold Bill to which allusion has been made in Chapter I.   The Act, as will have been noticed, contains one principle which is a particularly novel one.   The principle is that under which the County Council, on purchasing land from a landowner, and re-selling it to a small holder, may leave "a portion, not exceeding one-fourth of the purchase money," unpaid; the interest of which one-fourth may form a perpetual rent-charge on the holding, payable by the occupying cultivator to the Council.   In this way it will be apparent that the Council might become in the course of time the possessors of a valuable annual income from the various small holdings which their credit (in other words, the ratepayers') has secured for the small holders; and this income would go, of course, towards reducing the local burdens of the county.   The Council would, in fact (to use a colloquial expression), get a *quid pro quo* for whatever the risk might be which they had undertaken in the buying and re-selling of the land.   As regards the small holder, he (let it be well borne in mind), whether the Council decide that there shall be a small permanent rent-charge payable to them or not, becomes the absolute owner of his land for all cultivating purposes; he cannot be turned out of it, so long as he pays (1) the instalments of the purchase money as they become due, or (2) the small annual rent-charge; and he can devise or sell the land, in its entirety but not in portions, to whomsoever he chooses, for cultivating purposes.   Mr. Jesse Collings, instead of allowing only one-fourth of the purchase money to remain unpaid in the manner indicated, provided in his Bill for *three*-fourths, and we believe he still holds the opinion that this would have been preferable both to the small holder and to the County Council, inasmuch as, in addition to the increased advantage to the Council in the shape of permanent income, the three-fourths would have been a better security against the holder falling into the hands of the money-lender—an individual who has been ever ready to pounce down upon those whom he thinks he can (morally if not legally) swindle with the least trouble and with the best results to himself. Another advantage, too, would have been that having the three-fourths in question irredeemable (and at the lowest possible interest), the small holder would have so much the more money remaining with which to purchase stock and to cultivate the land.

CHAPTER VII.

THE COTTAGE AND FARM BUILDINGS DIFFICULTY.

LET us now return to what we were saying about the land-owners and the Act. They are, we stated, more and more welcoming it in theory; a few only in actual practice. The chief reason for the former is the cost of erection of suitable farm buildings for the holders—a point deserving, of course, serious consideration. This was brought out very clearly in the evidence before the Select Committee which inquired into the whole question of small holdings a few years ago. Lord Wantage said that on a holding of 50 acres the required buildings could be provided for "about £100." Mr. Squarey, a land-agent, declared that "the want of buildings" prohibited the creation of small holdings. Mr. Robertson stated that unless the proposed tenant has capital of his own, the question of the buildings becomes a "real difficulty." Mr. Alexander said that there is "considerable difficulty in the extension of small holdings, due to the heavy charge for providing buildings." Mr. Duncan declared that owners "do not cut up their estates into small farms because they cannot afford to put up the buildings."

It is clear, therefore, that the provision of suitable buildings was considered an overwhelming obstacle to the extension of the small holdings system. We cannot help thinking, however, that there is very much misconception by landlords on this point, as we hope to show.

We were led to pay a visit to the estate of a gentleman in the North of England, where the difficulty has been practically overcome. This gentleman is known for the considerable interest he takes in the allotments question, exemplified as it has long been by his having placed at the disposal of the labourers surrounding his estate, some 100 to 200 acres of land in one-acre plots. Of the three experimental small holdings set apart by that gentleman, we refer in detail to the buildings on one, the first created. The holding is some 17 acres in extent, but it should be noted that the whole structure provided is suitable for at least 25 acres. The total cost of its erection was only £35 14s. 2d., a sum lower by many pounds than is usually supposed. The materials used were as follow:—

	£	s.	d.
Timber, red deal (for sides and ends of building)	9	9	0
Roofing, corrugated galvanised iron	10	11	10
Blacksmith's charge making iron rods and bands for doors, etc.	3	13	6
Bricklayer (for foundation work)	2	9	10
Carpenter	3	10	0
Tar, 40 gallons	1	10	0
Fowlhouse	2	0	0
2,000 bricks	2	10	0
Total	£35	14	2

When we asked if he found the buildings to answer his

purpose, the small holder replied in a simple way, but without hesitation, "Yes, sir, very well; quite sufficient for all purposes." Upon measuring the structure, we found that it was 38 ft. by 30 ft. in size, and that it contained an open stockyard; a barn or store-room (12 ft. by 17 ft.); a covered yard (17 ft. by 18 ft.); and a cow-house, a calf-house, and a piggery, all covered, and measuring 6 ft. by 10 ft. in each case. The whole of the roofing

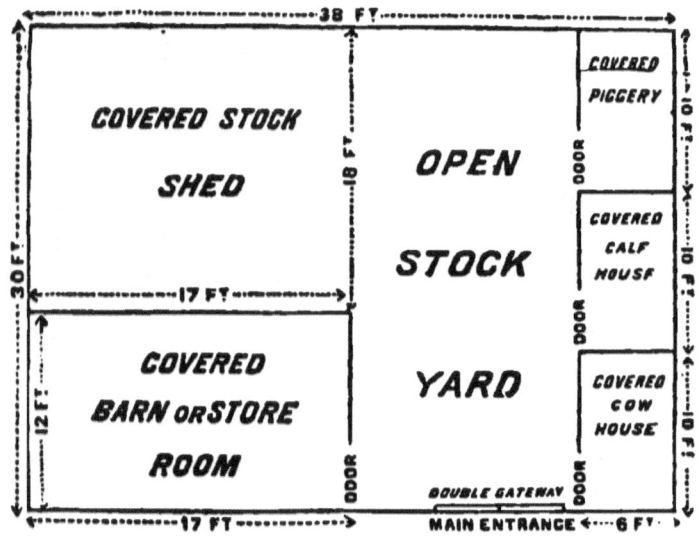

GROUND PLAN.

was of corrugated iron, and fixed in a slightly arched form.

The small holder was formerly a labourer; he was of a saving disposition, and so became a sort of higgler and haulier in a small way. His next step was to take the holding referred to, which, with the aid of a sensible and hard-working wife, he is conducting with much success. · He has no family; the holding is all arable; and we do not hesitate to say that, if such a specimen of a cultivating occupier, who has no special advantages as to markets, soil, or otherwise, could be largely increased in suitable districts, it would and must tend to the benefit of all classes of the community.

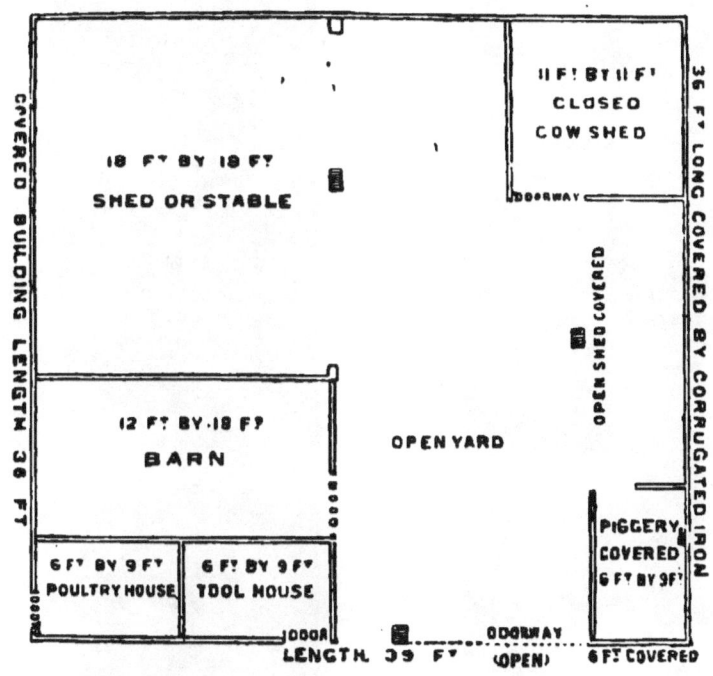

PLAN E.

We have also made numerous inquiries as to the cost of other suitable farm buildings made chiefly from galvanised iron, and suitable for a twenty to a twenty-five acre farm. The above illustration gives the ground plan of such building.

Plans F and G show the elevation of the last mentioned farm buildings (Plan E).

ELEVATION PLAN F.

ELEVATION PLAN G.

Plan F shows (1) the covered shed or stable, (2) the barn, and (3) the poultry and tool-houses.   Plan G shows (1) the closed cow-shed and door thereto, (2) the open-fronted shed, and (3) the piggery, each apartment being covered.

The price for these farm buildings delivered to any railway station within the following limits, *viz.*, from Hull (*via* Stafford) to Plymouth, and the country thereabouts (say the midland, southern, and eastern counties), is £47 10s. 0d. The roofs are covered with galvanised corrugated curved iron sheeting, 24 B.W.G. ; and the necessary rivets, screws, and washers, and timber framing (4 in. by 3 in., and 3 in. by 3 in.) are supplied, the whole being suitably mortised and tenoned together. There are five doors, with locks, hinges, etc., and one set of wrought-iron tie and King rods. The necessary sawn boards would have to be supplied by the purchaser, these being usually obtainable at a cheaper rate in the various localities. If the farm buildings are fixed by the vendor, the charge would be £11 11s. extra. The purchaser would be expected to do the cartage from his local station to the site, to dig and fill in the necessary holes, and to lend a little scaffolding.

The cost for the *alteration and repair* of buildings is, of course, greater where small holdings abound than where they do not. That, in addition to the cost of *erection*, forms one of the arguments of landlords against cutting up their estates. From a landlord's point of view, the objection may be, and from the point of view of an impecunious or encumbered landlord is in reality, serious ; but we are certain from what we know of the rural classes, the objection is one upon which owners of land need feel very little alarm. Those who desire small holdings would themselves do much in the way of alteration and repair, which upon a larger holding would certainly not always be done by the tenant.

The visit, however, and other inquiries to which we have referred, convinced us that if landowners only knew of the comparatively trivial expense, in actual practice, of erecting suitable farm buildings, they would not hesitate to adopt the small holdings system, and to give it at least a fair trial. The sum of £35 14s. 2d., or even £50 or £60, is almost ridiculously small if it will enable a landlord to erect the necessary building accommodation for a 25-acre or a 30-acre holding.

Where a small holder is granted a few acres of land, he would, indeed, in many instances, find little or no difficulty in himself attending to and satisfactorily settling this farm buildings question for himself, as has been done before now. A man with, say, a dozen acres near a small town would not (and has been known not to) find much trouble in hiring premises in the town until such time as he could erect others on his holding; or, in other cases, he would find little inconvenience or difficulty in erecting on his holding or adjoining his cottage some little shelter, hovel, or out-building, which would answer all his requirements until such time as he could make other more suitable arrangements.

But the provision of *cottages* has also been considered an obstacle. It must not be forgotten that with thousands of farms there are cottages which go with the land. The land is, nowadays, too often only half cultivated, and the labourers in many instances are idle most of their time through having no work to do. It is submitted that in such a case and without any injury whatever to the farmer, these men, many of whom are most thrifty and capable, might be assisted on to portions of the land which their employer is unable properly to cultivate. There is, some will say, still a difficulty about the *farmers'* buildings. What is to become of *them?* They will, it is argued, go to ruin. The reply is the sooner the better if the keeping of them in repair is the only alternative to poverty or starvation on the part of the workpeople. We were in a small midland village not long ago. One of the farmers a few years since employed ten to twelve men. He now employs a man and a youth. Another farmer in the same place constantly employed and still employs nine men and a youth, *i.e.*, as many as the farm will give work to. Where are the cottages and the discharged men in the former case? The cottages and the farmers' land are where they were. The men, however, are gone; but they ought to be on the land, even at the expense of the farmers' buildings. We could multiply similar instances. We cite one other only. It relates to a Northamptonshire village, the able-bodied labourers in which, to the number of about fifty, used to find daily employment on farms in the parish. Most of the arable land has now been laid down to pasture, so much so that nearly thirty of the men have to seek work out of the village. To secure this the poor fellows must walk one, two and three miles or more both morning and night, and often on the mere chance of being successful in their quest. This, again, it is submitted, is not a right state of affairs, and it is absurd to say that either the question of cottages— which exist in abundance about the village—or the question of the farm buildings, which would be too large or become unused (they are that already), should stand in the way of altering such an unsatisfactory state of things.

We are convinced that the "cottage question" is far less a difficulty than the opponents of small holdings seek to make out, and we are equally convinced that those who have a real desire to establish the system—to give it a fair trial—have only to look the facts concerning it in the face in order to overcome any scruples they may have on the particular point to which we refer.

Our experience, moreover, is that the small holder does not object to walk what some of us would deem a considerable distance, so long as he can procure a few acres of ground—so great is his eagerness for the latter. Cottages may usually be found within what the eager small holder would consider not too great a distance to walk or, maybe, to ride, for, at any rate, a time ; and it must not be for-

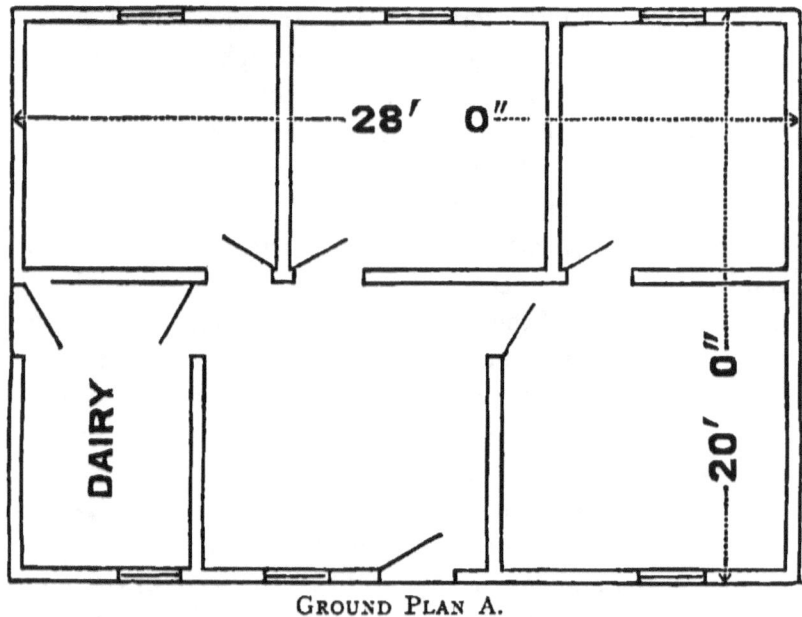

GROUND PLAN A.

gotten, too, that where the thrifty and intelligent are given a start on to the land, they will, in nine cases out of ten, overcome many of those obstacles which appear to us insuperable, and overcome them, too, in a manner as astonishing as it is praiseworthy. The tenant will do himself that which on a larger holding has to be done by the estate carpenter, the village blacksmith, or other local man ; and he will do it all the more readily, we may be sure, if he can feel that his tenure is secure, or that the land he occupies is his own.

We have, however, on this particular point as to cottages also made numerous inquiries, with the result that well-built, substantial cottages, chiefly of galvanised material, can be erected at what must be admitted is a very reasonable figure indeed. We give illustrations and estimates which we have had prepared of (1) a six-roomed cottage ; and (2) a four-roomed cottage.

The ground plan (A) and the elevation (B) are of the larger cottage.

This cottage is 28 ft. long over all ; 20 ft. wide over all ; 9 ft. high to eaves ; 16 ft. high to ridge.

ELEVATION PLAN B.

The cottage is formed with strong timber, mortised and tenoned together. The roof, sides, and ends are covered with galvanised corrugated iron sheeting, with the necessary galvanised rivets, nails, washers, and ridge capping. It is lined with boarding and felting, and has one inch planed, tongued, and grooved flooring boards throughout. The necessary gutters and spouts are also provided. The cost of this would be about £103, delivered, as before, to any railway station within the following limits, *viz.*, from Hull (*via* Stafford) to Plymouth, and the country thereabouts (say the midland, eastern, and southern counties). The additional cost of labour in erecting on brick foundations found by the purchaser, or into the ground, would be £37.

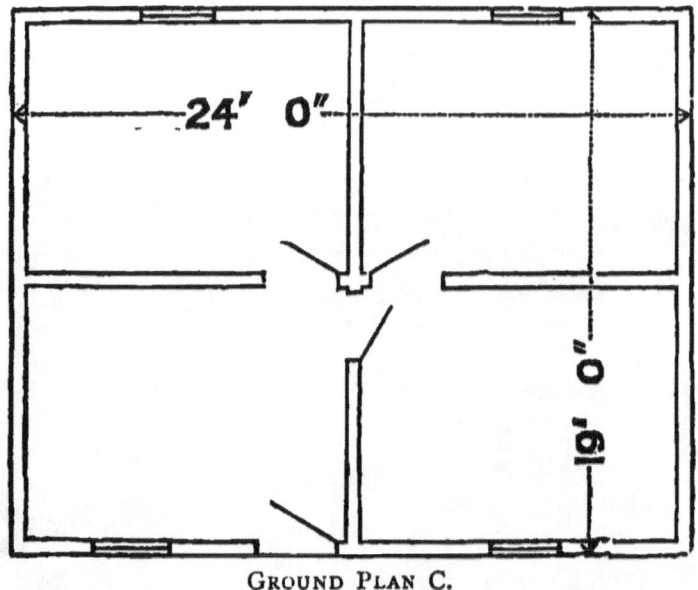

GROUND PLAN C.

The next two illustrations show the ground plan (C) and elevation (D) of the smaller cottage.

The size is 24 ft. long over all; 19 ft. wide over all; 9 ft. high to eaves; 15 ft. high to ridge.

The price in this case, delivered as before mentioned, would be £85 10s.; with an additional sum of £27 10s. for erecting as above mentioned.

No sum is stated for a porch or a privy. In each case this would come to £4, with £4 4s. extra if erected by the vendor. The foregoing figures exclude certain small charges for cartage from the purchaser's station to the site; and also for digging and filling in the holes if the erections were to be fixed into the ground.

A suitable stove, with the necessary piping, etc., for

ELEVATION PLAN D.

heating and cooking purposes, can be had at prices ranging up to £5. If necessary, the inside of each cottage could be packed along the galvanised material with any loose material, for the purpose of supplying extra warmth in winter.

For the guidance of those owners who, having the means, may either now or in the future desire to erect more substantial farm buildings and cottages than those we have described, we give some illustrations and details of struc-

F

tures put up by Lord Kinnaird on his Rossie estate, with which illustrations and details we have, by request of his lordship, been favoured through his lordship's agent.

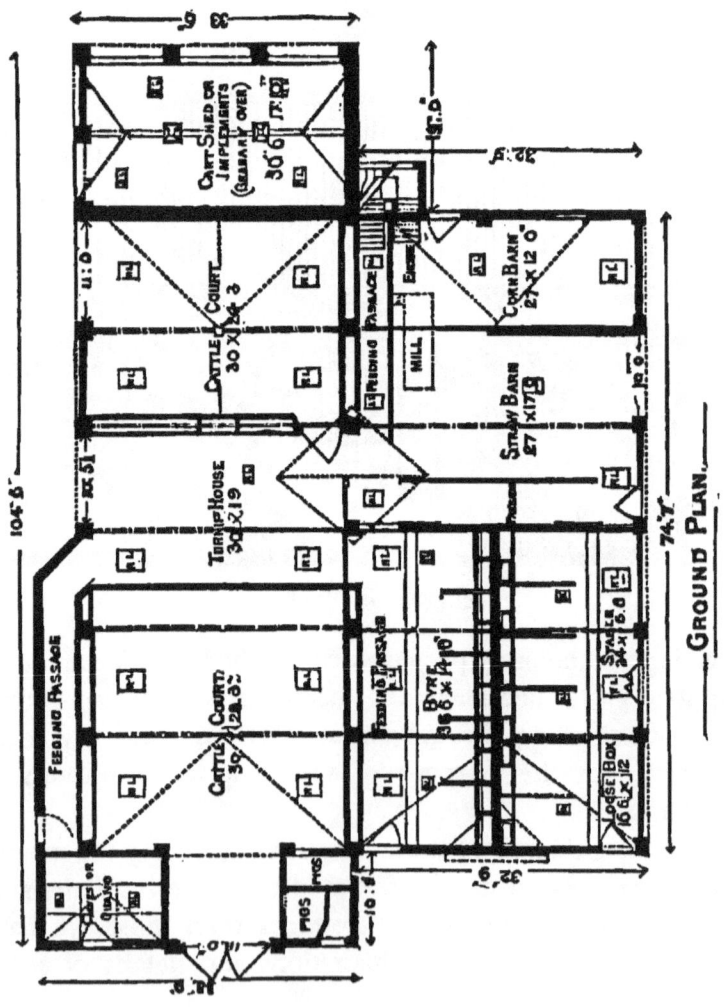

A farm of over 270 acres becoming vacant, and the existing steading, situated towards the north end of the farm, not

being sufficiently commodious for modern wants, it was
decided to divide the farm into three smaller holdings of
75, 70, and 121 acres respectively—the 70 and 121-acre
farms getting the existing steading divided between them,
a dwelling-house being provided in a convenient position
for the former, and the old farm-house going with the latter.
The large modern farm-house, erected some years ago for the
entire farm, together with five acres of land, it was proposed
to let separately.   On the 75 acres near the south end
of the original farm, the buildings shown have been
erected and named " Exton " by Lady Kinnaird.   In de-
signing these buildings the object in view has been to provide a maximum of covered accommodation at a minimum
of cost, without at the same time reducing the permanence
and stability of the structure as a whole.   The nearest
working stone quarry being fully four miles distant, and the
heavy cartage of stone for walls being a serious element in
the cost, it was decided to erect the steading in concrete,
and the house in brickwork.   The steading, it will be observed, consists mostly of pillars, with 6-in. walls between,
about 5 ft. high, the space over being in some parts closed
in with close-jointed flooring boards fixed to the wall-plate
above, and to the runner on top of 6-in. wall ; the divisions
of turnip-house, and between centre pillars, are of flooring
boards, having thin concrete foundation walls carried above
ground level.   The sides of passages by the straw-house are
of open woodwork, and have upright ladders for convenient
access to the lofts above from stable and byres.   The
pillars were constructed by temporarily fastening three
concrete building frames together to form three sides, and
setting these on end, leaving the third side open to allow
the concrete to be filled in, this side being closed by short
boards across, and nailed on from time to time as the

building rose.   The concrete was composed of small whinstone material, gravel size, from the estate stone-breaking

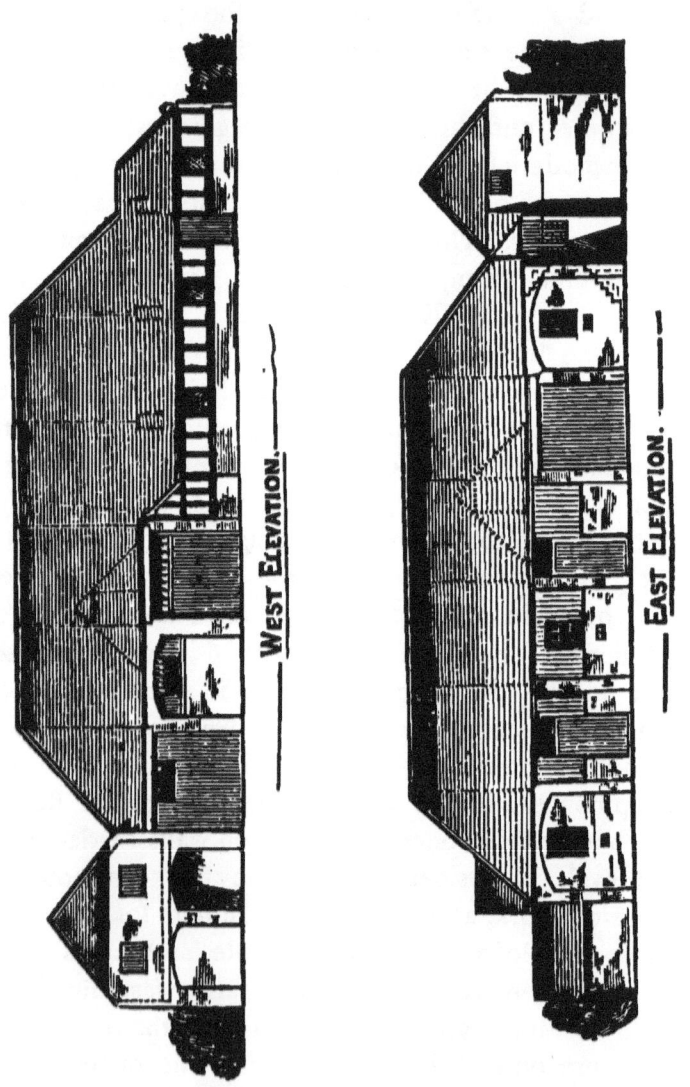

machine—the fine dust having been previously sifted out
by the machine riddle—mixed in the proportion of seven

of this material to one of cement. The pillars and concrete walls were packed with large whinstones, the concrete being well rammed down the sides of the frame. The stable floor and floor of byre from feeding-trough to channel are cause-wayed, and paved with whinstone from the estate quarry, and the stable divisions are of whitewood 6½ in. by 2½ in., held by heel posts of channel steel bedded in concrete at the floor and bolted to joists at the roof. The troughs are of fire-clay and haiks of larchwood. The byre divisions and troughs are of concrete finished smooth ; the channel and passage of byre are of concrete left somewhat rough, and the other passages and floors are of clay. The walls of byres, stable, and corn - room have been plastered with cement on the inside four feet in height, and plastered above with one coat of lime plaster. It was intended that a mill should have been placed near the boiler-house, but as the lofts in the roof are very ample, and it is intended for the first few years to use the district travelling threshers to deliver the straw direct into the lofts, this has not been carried out. The roofs are covered with boarding ⅝ in. thick, half-way up the rafters, creosoted pine lath being put on the top half. The granary roof is wholly boarded and covered with strong felt under the slates. The whole roofs of steading are of P.D. Welsh slating open bond.

The site of the dwelling-houses being on clay, the founda-tions to the level of sleeper joists are of concrete, packed with stones, and with a damp course of slates in cement. The external walls above are 15 in. thick, of hollow brick-work, held by galvanised iron wall-ties with turn-down points. Mantel grates, with fire-brick backs, have been fixed in all the rooms, the wash-tub and sink are of en-amelled fire-clay, and the shelves of the dairy are slate. The stair is of pitch pine, and the roof is covered with felt and P.D. close slating. The outside of the walls of house and steading has been plastered throughout with cement plaster, mixed with dry red oxide of iron paint, which gives a pleasing effect. Water has been taken by 2-in. iron pipes a distance of over 400 yards from the gravitation supply made some years ago from the hills to all the Carse

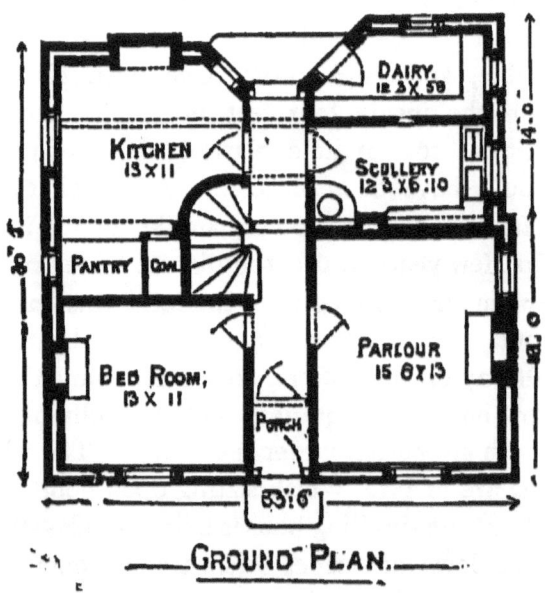

GROUND PLAN.

farms on Rossie estate, and water is put into the cattle courts. It was intended to erect a water-trough at the south-east corner of the steading for the horses. A small out-house for boiler and coals, and house privy were still to be erected, and the whole drainage has been taken a little to the east to a 15-in. pipe drain 12 ft. deep, carried up from the River Tay about twenty years ago to drain this part of the estate. A modification of this plan, and one which would lessen the cost very much in proportion, could be made by having the cart-shed and granary in the space occupied by the inside cattle-court on the north side of the turnip-house.

The whole of the concrete-work has been executed by four estate labourers and a plasterer ; the materials used in concrete and cement plaster-work were 41 tons of cement,

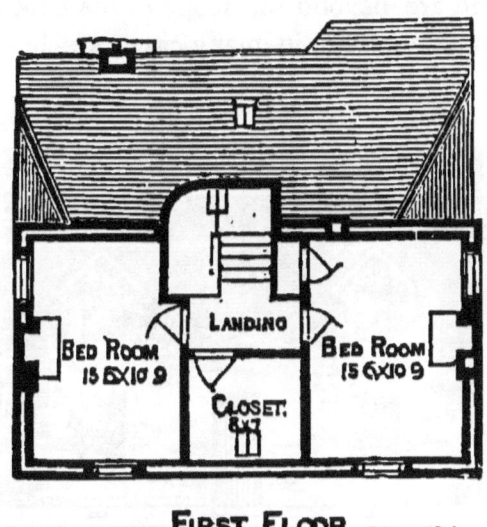

FIRST FLOOR.

202 loads of small material, 72 loads of packing stones, and about 12 loads of sand. The plumber and joiner work have been satisfactorily executed by experienced tradesmen on the estate; the other works were mostly done by contract, and the whole was met by a cost of about £650.

These farms readily secured tenants, who, it may be added, were not those who offered the highest rent, but such as were well known, industrious, and careful men of the neighbourhood, and of good reputation.   The tenants of Exton and of the 121 acres farm were both experienced farm grieves, and that of the 70 acres farm a successful contractor from a neighbouring village.

It may, however, be urged that even the expenses of the cheaper farm buildings and cottages to which we have alluded are beyond the scope of the bulk of the landowners nowadays, who, in many cases, are but tenants for

SOUTH ELEVATION.

life, and who have absolutely no available funds after the necessary expenditure on annual repairs and other fixed annual charges are provided for.   In such cases, and they are, unfortunately, far more numerous than the general public is aware of, we do not hesitate to say that the State should come to the rescue.

The system of advancing money to Irish landowners has been pursued with considerable advantage all round ; and what is done in Ireland in such a matter as this might well be done in England in the case of English landowners—especially in the case of the smaller landowners. In return for advances enabling them to erect farm buildings and cottages for small holdings purposes, they might be called upon to—and they willingly would, we believe—submit[1] to certain limitations or restrictions, during repayment of the monies, on the rent to be asked, and, of course, the landlords would also be held responsible for keeping the structures in repair.

As to whether small holdings will really prove remunerative to the occupiers of them, we do not think it necessary to discuss the question. We have proved it over and over again. It is certain that large farms, speaking generally, are not profitable either to the occupiers or to those dependent upon them ; whereas, given a fair chance both as to situation and as to the right men being put into them, small holdings in England have stood the test of the depression in agriculture during the recent past better than large holdings. Remember we are not arguing for the cutting up of all large farms into small ones. To thus argue would be ridiculous in the eyes of practical men, and the attempt, if carried out in practice, would result in failure and disaster. It would be absurd to cut up a large hill sheep farm, for instance, which is practically fit for nothing else but sheep feeding and breeding. No : what is argued for is that small holdings should be much more numerous in *suitable* localities, of which there are thousands upon thousands in this country. The desirability of small holdings has been recognised, as we have intimated, by the State, and what we have now to do—what, in fact, we have attempted to do—is to show what the legislative machinery is, and how it can be carried out in practice.

---

[1] Sir Michael Hicks-Beach has expressed such sentiments.

Although, as already stated, we do not deem it necessary to discuss the question as to whether small holdings would be remunerative, it may, nevertheless, be interesting if we cite two or three cases of successful holders. Here is one personally known to us.

Mr. B—— is thirty-nine years of age, and occupies 15 acres of land, of which he owns one and rents 14. He is married, and has twelve children—six boys and six girls. The three eldest are girls, the fourth child being a boy close upon sixteen years of age. The eldest girl is in her twenty-first year. Mr. B—— grows fruit principally (strawberries and raspberries), the other crops being vegetables of various kinds. He does not grow any straw crops at all, but he grows about half an acre of grass to assist in feeding his horse. In addition to this he has two pigs, and some 50 head of poultry. Sometimes the number of sow pigs which he keeps is six, seven, or eight, the litters being sold off when they are young.

Mr. B—— is the son of a boot and shoe maker, and started life in the same trade, under his father, as soon as he could toddle about. He left that trade at the early age of eleven, taking to farm labouring and blacksmithing, as a journeyman workman, until about his twenty-fifth year, when he took to nail-making and gardening jointly, making his nails in an ordinary labourer's cottage on his own account. By much perseverance, thrift, and care, he was able gradually to extend his allotment ground, and whilst doing this he decreased his labour as a nailer, which was becoming, as now, more and more an extinct trade, and unprofitable withal. As an allotment holder, he started with a quarter acre of ground, which he increased to half an acre, and then to one acre. Bit by bit he increased the size of his holding, until at the present time he occupies no less than 15 acres. Mr. B—— is a typical son of the soil, both as regards appearance and robustness of health : he has "money in the bank," and he intends to add, as soon as he can procure them, another 10 to 20 acres to his 15.

Mr. C—— of Cambridgeshire had 12 acres of land, to which four more acres were subsequently added. He and his family have obtained their living by this land, and have never had anything else to depend upon.

Mr. D—— began as a labourer with a house and a garden at £7 a year rent. He is at the present moment farming about 20 acres, and does very little in the way of extraneous work, nor has he any need to. He has four cottages and gardens which he has bought with his own money.

Mr. E—— began with one acre, and now has 20. Not only does he seem able to buy almost anything in the way of stock, but he could, we are informed, put down any day £200 in such purchases if he desired to do so. He kills a large number of sheep weekly, together with seven or eight pigs.

Mr. F—— has had six acres of land—having five now. He has got on so well that he keeps a horse and cart, and lives entirely on his small piece of ground.

Lastly :—The following are the balance-sheets of two small holders. The first relates to a holding of five acres, the tenant having also a "run" of about nine acres of wood; and the second relates to a holding of 14 acres 1 rood 31 poles. Both holdings are in Montgomeryshire, a county which may be considered as one of small properties, and by no means offering any exceptional facilities to the holders. The two balance-sheets—according to the land-

lord who owns the land tenanted by the holders—may be
taken as typical instances of others in the county :—

(a)

To stock—							
Two cows at £14,	...	...	£28	0	0		
Four ewes at 35s.,	...	...	7	0	0		
One sow,	...	...	...	2	0	0	
Fowls, ...	...	...	...	3	0	0	
						£40 0 0	
To rent, ...	...	...	...	...	...	9 12 0	
,, land tax and tithe,	...	...	...	...	0 14 3	
,, poor rates,	...	...	...	...	...	0 13 0	
,, feeding stuffs for pigs and fowls,	...	...	8 0 0	
,, balance (profit),	...	...	...	...	28 13 9	
						£87 13 0	

By sale of 320lb. of butter at 1s.,	...	...	£16	0	0	
,, ,, two calves,	...	...	...	...	4	0	0
,, ,, eleven pigs at 15s.,	...	...	...	8	5	0
,, ,, six lambs at 28s.,	...	...	...	8	8	0
,, ,, poultry,	...	..	...	...	12	0	0
,, stock, *viz.* :—						
Two cows at £13,	...	...	£26	0	0	
Sow, ...	...	...	...	2	0	0	
Ewes, ...	...	...	...	8	0	0	
Fowls, ...	...	...	...	3	0	0	
						39 0 0	
						£87 13 0	

The above small holder adds to his income by doing garden
work for neighbours in the summer, and by killing pigs in the
winter.   He estimates the value of butter, butter milk, skim
milk, fruit, and vegetables consumed in his household at
£6 16s.

(*b*)

To rent, ...	£28	5	0
„ tithe, ...	2	0	0
„ poor rates and land tax, ...	2	10	0
	£32	15	0
Balance (profit), ...	31	5	0
	£64	0	0

By sale from stock, etc., of one cow, yearly,	£13	0	0
„ sale of one yearling, ...	8	0	0
„ „ one calf, ...	2	0	0
„ „ sow and pigs, ...	8	0	0
„ „ butter, ...	13	0	0
„ „ fat pigs, ...	3	0	0
„ „ poultry, ...	2	0	0
„ milk and butter consumed at home, ...	10	0	0
„ apples, potatoes, and vegetables do., ...	5	0	0
	£64	0	0

In this case the small holder has sufficient spare time to add "considerably" to his income by working elsewhere. The value of the live stock on the holding was £61, composed of three cows (£39); two yearlings (£16); one sow (£3); and poultry (£3).

These several instances may be taken as typical of many other successful small holders who have no very special facilities as to proximity to markets, soil, competition, etc., not possessed by the larger farmers.

CHAPTER VIII.

COUNTY COUNCILS AND SMALL FARMS.

WE cannot conclude our references to the question of small holdings without expressing the hope that the County Councils will do all they can to put the Small Holdings Act into operation. It is true that without the landlord's consent to the creation of small holdings in any particular locality the County Councils cannot place any person or persons in the possession of any such holdings. The various Councils can, however, foster public opinion upon the small holdings question throughout their counties, as some few have, by the circulation of leaflets relating to the Act, etc. And, what is more, they should view with a considerable degree of sympathy the petitions for small holdings, which will certainly come more and more numerously before them as time goes on. We do not mean that the ratepayers' money should be seriously risked out of a sympathetic regard for the would-be small holders. We do mean that when such men—men who are of good character, well known in their respective districts, honest, thrifty, intelligent, and capable—appeal to them for land on which they may push forward in a career which, so far, they have made a success of, they should use every effort to accomplish the wish dearest to those men's hearts—a wish the State has itself declared is one which on public grounds should, and ought to, be satisfied.

Instances have been brought under our observation

where County Councils have not adopted this attitude, and some in which they have been impatient and even hostile to the petitioners.

It is, however, interesting to mention, in this connection, that one County Council in particular has recently purchased and set apart 147 acres for small holdings purposes. This is the Worcestershire Council, and the district in which the land is situate is Catshill. In conjunction with the Right Honourable Jesse Collings, M.P., and Mr. Councillor Frank Smith (President and Honorary Secretary respectively of the Rural Labourers' League of Birmingham), we had a good deal to do in assisting the men, and in negotiating on their behalf with the County Council for this land, as well as in assisting a very great number of men in many parts of the same district and county to obtain allotments; and we may say that thus far we look back on the various results with absolute and unqualified satisfaction. We give below an account of the whole matter as described in the Birmingham *Daily Mail* of July 3rd, 1895. This will show what those who wrote it (unknown to ourselves) think of the Small Holdings and Allotment Movement in the county in question. We express the hope that this account may act as an encouragement to many councillors in other parts who may happen to read it.

" Within the past five years or so the strawberry crop within a radius of ten miles of Birmingham has increased enormously. That increase is nearly all due to the creation of allotments under Mr. Jesse Collings's Acts of 1887 and 1890. Put in so many words, this may not appeal to the city dweller as a fact of mighty importance. Strawberries at 3d. or 4d. a pound are very nice, but they are not essential to the life and happiness of the people within whose reach they are placed at these low prices. That is true in a sense. But let us look at the other side of the picture ; let us put on one side altogether the good which a cheap supply of wholesome fruit does to a teeming population like ours, a great good by the way, and let us seek to grasp the benefit this strawberry growing has conferred on the cultivator. With this aim the writer spent the early hours of Monday morning among the strawberry gatherers on the Catshill allotments. He got on the scene at half-past five o'clock, but the gardeners had been at work quite two hours before that, and the first waggonload of fruit, made up of 100 boxes, containing 12lb. of strawberries each, was just leaving the ground for the Birmingham market. The sight from the brow of the big 43-acre field was one that spoke in eloquent tones to anyone that knew what Catshill was a few years ago. The village, which lies within the Urban district of North Bromsgrove parish, is peopled with that most miserable of toilers, the nailers. The little cottages clustered round the church in the valley looked cheerful and gay in the early morning sun, and formed a lovely background to the great allotment field, at the extreme end of which we were now standing. Every one of these cottages had its little workshop attached, the workshop in which the father, the mother, and the children, down to the toddler of five and six years, were forced to toil all day long at nail-making, in order to earn a bare subsistence. That was before the allotments were created, when the field which now stretched at our feet down to the village was in pasture, and was occupied by a few cattle. This morning, however, it is a very different sight we see. There is no smoke from the nail forges, not a hearth fire in the village is alight, not a sound from a single hammer is to be heard from one end of Catshill to the other. Instead of working at the nailing forge, the whole population, men

women and children, are spread over the allotments in this
43-acre field on which we are looking, and they are all
picking strawberries for the Birmingham market. Three
hundred gatherers, all busy, and everyone of them nailers.
We stroll down the waggon track and get among these
allotment holders and strawberry pickers, and find them a
bright-faced, well-fared, contented lot of people, happy in
their work, and ambitious to get on. What a contrast this
to what used to be. Six years ago these same people of
Catshill made one sad to look on them. Their thin,
pinched faces then bore the stolid look of despair. They
were the worst paid and hardest wrought artisans in the
whole of England. The lot of the Catshill nailer was
blank misery.

"The fact is that the Allotments Acts of 1887 and
1890 have saved Catshill from starvation by creating a
new industry. The way in which these strawberry
gardens were brought into existence affords a very char-
acteristic instance of the difficulties to be met with in
putting the people on the land. The Urban Sanitary
Authority which ruled Catshill six years ago was composed
entirely of farmers, whose sole actuating idea was to keep
down the rates. To accomplish this they neglected the
roads, and so raised the ire of the villa residents round
Barnt Green and Blackwell. Two of these residents, Mr.
Frank Smith and Mr. Bigwood, took the matter up, and
when they began to agitate among the nailmakers of Catshill they soon had their eyes opened to another matter
which the farmers in authority were neglecting, *viz.*, the demand of the poor nailers for allotment land. The farmers
refused to listen to any representation, so it ended in
Messrs. Smith and Bigwood being nominated and returned
as members of the Urban Sanitary Authority, pledged

G

to support a petition for allotments from the Catshill
nailers. This took the farmers so much by surprise that
they yielded to the new members. Fortunately, a land-
owner was found who was willing to let land for
allotments at a moderate rent. It had been the custom among the landowners of the district to charge
three times the rent for allotment land, compared
with that charged for ordinary farming. The field of 43
acres, which the Authority were able to rent, had been let
to the outgoing farmer for something less than £1 an acre.
The Authority got it for 30s. an acre, and were able to let
it out in allotments varying from a quarter of an acre to
two acres, from £1 to two guineas an acre, according to
the quality of the land. The seventy lots were taken up at
once, the apportionment being by ballot. The tenancies
began on Lady Day, 1891, and there has never been an
allotment vacant from that day to this. The nailers cleaned
the ground, which was very filthy, with potatoes the first
season, and got a crop which, on the average, paid them a
profit of about £3 an acre. Then they planted the land
with strawberries, and have gone on prospering more and
more each year. These 43 acres, when in pasture six years
ago, could not be made to pay. To-day they have raised
seventy families in Catshill from a state of something akin
to starvation to one of comfort and contentment. An acre of
strawberries at Catshill in a fair season is worth about £50 to
the grower. Last week an acre allotment holder took £21
13s. worth of fruit off his ground. It costs about 4d. a
dozen pounds to gather and market the fruit, and the
average price which the grower is getting this season may be
taken at 2s. a dozen pounds. Half the return may be taken
as profit; that means that the Catshill allotment holders
make £25 a year out of each acre. When the land was

secured, the farmers said it was a shame to cut up old pasture, but to-day the field is worth £500 a year more than it was five years ago. That is what allotments have done for Catshill.

"The cry now is for more land, so the County Council decided to put into operation the Small Holdings Act of 1892, which the late Unionist Government passed at the instigation of Mr. Jesse Collings. A petition was presented to the County Council for powers under the Act, Mr. Frank Smith, through the Rural Labourers' League, of which he is a prominent official, stating the case on behalf of the villagers. The County Council Committee held that a case had been made out for the Act to be put into operation, and as the result they bought the 'Woodrow' Farm, which adjoins the allotment ground, for the purpose of laying it out in small holdings. This farm is 147 acres in extent, and the price paid for it is £4,900. The County Council are now mapping it out into small holdings of from two to seven acres, and applications are rapidly coming in. It is believed that the Council will be able to sell the land at about £43 an acre, so as to cover interest and sinking fund on the loan. The small holder has to pay a fifth of the purchase money down, and it is calculated that for a small holding costing £100, after the £20 pound deposit is paid, the small holder's payment will only be about £1 13s. each half-year for fifty years. This is just about the rent which the allotment holders in Catshill are paying, so that the man who can save sufficient to put down the necessary fifth of the purchase money for a small holding, is placed in a position of being able to acquire his land in fifty years by paying a very moderate rent.

"There is thus a prospect of the poor, down-trodden

nailmakers of Catshill, whose future was so desperate six years ago, becoming prosperous owners of small holdings. It is a wonderfully beneficent change for these people, a striking example of what can be done by a wise enforcement of the Acts for putting the labourer on the land, which were passed by the late Government."

In two or three counties besides Worcestershire, the Small Holdings Act has been put into operation on a small scale by the Councils of them ; but its application is by no means as general yet as it is destined in time to become.

PART III.—UNEMPLOYED AND THE LAND.

CHAPTER IX.

THE TOWN UNEMPLOYED AND THE LAND: AND MUNICIPAL FARMING.

THE past four or five years have been productive of many suggestions for placing the town unemployed upon the land. These suggestions have, amongst some recognised leaders of labour, culminated in the demand that the unemployed should, under the provisions of certain ancient Statutes, be set to work, with or without wages. We have carefully examined this demand, and have also examined and compared the ancient enactments with the view of seeing whether the latter could be utilised as desired by those who have been assiduous in placing the demand in question before the public. It may be remembered by those interested in the matter that the demand has been made upon the Local Government Board: who, it was and still is urged, could and should issue certain " rules, orders, and regulations " to effect the object in view.

We give below all the necessary details of the Acts relied upon—as well as a resumé thereof—in order to see what chance there is of the Acts being made available for the purpose in hand :—

During the reign of Elizabeth the famous Act was passed (in 1601, cap. 2), entitled " An Act for the Relief of the

Poor." Section 1 provides that the churchwardens and
overseers "shall" set to work children of all such whose
parents be thought by the overseers unable to keep and maintain them.   The churchwardens and overseers, by the same
clause, "shall" set to work all persons, married or un-
married, having no means of maintaining themselves, and
who use no ordinary and daily trade of life to get their
living by.   Moreover, the overseers "shall" also raise,
weekly or otherwise, by taxation of every inhabitant, "a
convenient stock of flax, hemp, wool, thread, iron, and
other necessary ware and stuff to set the poor to work."
They were to raise "competent sums of money for and
towards the necessary relief of the lame, impotent, old,
blind, and such other among them being poor and not able
to work."   Finally, by the same clause, they were to raise
"money in a similar way for putting out of such children to
be apprentices, to be gathered out of the same parish
according to the ability of the same parish."   Section 2
provides that the churchwardens and overseers should meet
monthly in the church, on Sunday afternoon, after service,
"there to consider of some good course to be taken."   In
default of so meeting they were to pay 20s.   Section 3
provides that if the particular parish is not able to raise
sufficient money for the above purposes for its own requirements, two justices of the peace might "tax, rate, and assess
any other of other parishes, or out of any parish, within the
hundred where the said parish is;" and the money raised
was to be paid to the churchwardens and overseers "of the
poor parish" for the purposes indicated in section 1.
If the hundred was not thought by the justices fit to relieve
the poor parishes unable to provide for themselves, "then
the justices of the peace, at their general quarter sessions, or
the greater number of them, shall rate, or assess as aforesaid,

any other of other parishes, or out of any parish within the said county, for the purposes aforesaid, as in their discretion shall seem fit." Section 4 provides that in case the money is not duly paid up by those who are taxed or assessed, it shall be obtained "by distress and sale of the offenders' goods." "In defect of such distress," the offenders might be committed to gaol indefinitely. Section 5 provides that those persons apprenticed as aforesaid might, by the church-wardens and overseers, be bound until twenty-four years of age in the case of males, and until twenty-one in the case of females, or to the time of the marriage of the latter. This section also declares that "to the intent that necessary places of habitation may more conveniently be provided for such poor, impotent people . . . it shall be lawful for the churchwardens and overseers, by the leave of the lord and lords of the manor, whereof any waste or common within their parish is or shall be parcelled, to erect, build, or set up . . . in such waste or common at the general charges of the parish, or otherwise of the hundred or county, convenient houses of dwelling for the said impotent poor ; and also to place inmates or more families than one in one cottage or house." It also declared that such "cottages and places for inmates" should not be "used or employed to or for any other habitation, but only for the impotent and poor of the same parish that shall be there placed from time to time by the churchwardens and overseers." Section 6 provides that the justices at their quarter sessions might consider appeals from those who thought themselves over-taxed. Section 7 provides that "the father and grandfather, mother and grandmother, and the children of every poor old, blind, lame, and impotent person, or other poor person not able to work, being of sufficient ability, shall, at their own charges, relieve and maintain every such poor person in that manner, and according to that rate as by the justices of the peace of that county, where such sufficient persons dwell, or the greater number of them, at their general quarter sessions shall be assessed." The penalty of non-compliance with this was 20s. for every month "which they shall fail." Section 8 provides that overseers of corporate towns were to have the same authority within their jurisdiction as county justices of the peace. Section 9 refers to parishes which may extend into more counties than one. Sections 10 and 11 provide for a monetary forfeiture (to go towards the relief of the poor) by the justices of the peace in case there is no annual nomination of overseers for the work referred to. Section 12 provides that the justices of the peace shall rate every parish to a weekly sum as they shall think convenient. "No parish to be rated above 6d. or less than $\frac{1}{2}$d. ;" nor was the total amount of the taxation of the several parishes in the county to be above 2d. for every parish within the said county. Section 13 provides a penalty for refusing to pay the money which the parishioners were taxed or assessed to pay. Section 14 provides for the application of certain sums received from the taxation towards the relief of certain poor prisoners "of the King's Bench," and also to such hospitals and almshouses as shall be in the county. Section 15 provides for the application of surplus monies arising out of such taxation as aforesaid. Section 16 states the penalty for refusing to act as treasurer of monies received under section 14. Sections 17, 18, 19, and 20 are of no particular moment.

George III., 1819, March 31, cap. 12. On this date an Act was passed " to Amend the Laws for the Relief of the Poor." Section 1 provides for the constitution of a " Select Vestry " for the concerns of the poor of the parish, to meet every fourteen days, or oftener if necessary. The

vestry was "required" to examine into the state and condition of the poor of the parish, and also to inquire into
and determine "upon the proper objects of relief, and the
nature and amount of relief to be given; and in each case
shall take into consideration the character and conduct of
the poor to be relieved, and shall be at liberty to dis-
tinguish, in the relief to be granted, between the deserving
and the idle, extravagant or profligate poor." The vestry
was to make orders in writing for such relief as they
thought requisite. The overseers were required to con-
form to the directions of the select vestry, and were not to
give any other relief than that directed by the said vestry.
Section 2 provides for a power of appeal to a justice of the
peace in case of inadequate relief being granted. It also
provides that a justice of the peace may make an order for
relief of any case of urgent necessity. (This, however, was
repealed by a subsequent statute.) Section 12, after reciting that the Act of Elizabeth (already referred to)
"directed churchwardens and overseers to set to work
certain persons therein described," and that "by the laws
now in force there are not sufficient powers given to the
churchwardens and overseers to enable them to keep such
persons fully and constantly employed," went on to declare
"that it should be lawful for the churchwardens and overseers of the poor of any parish, with the consent of the inhabitants thereof in vestry assembled, to take into their
hands any land or ground which shall belong to such
parish, or to the churchwardens and overseers of the poor
of such parish, or to the poor thereof, or to purchase, or to
hire, and take on lease for, and on account of the parish,
any suitable portion or portions of land within or near to
such parish, not exceeding 20 acres in the whole; and to
employ and to set to work in the cultivation of such land,

on account of the parish, any such persons as by law they are
directed to set to work, and to pay to such of the poor
persons so employed as shall be supported by the parish,
reasonable wages for their work ; and the poor persons so
employed shall have such and the like remedies for the recovery of their wages, and shall be subject to such and the
like punishment for misbehaviour in their employment as
other labourers in husbandry are by law entitled and subject to." Section 13 provides "that for the promotion of
industry amongst the poor, it shall be lawful for the churchwardens and overseers of the poor of any parish, with the
consent of the inhabitants in vestry assembled, to let any
portion and portions of such parish land as aforesaid, or of
the land to be so purchased or taken on account of the
parish, to any poor and industrious inhabitant of the parish,
to be by him or her occupied and cultivated on his or her
own account, and for his or her own benefit, at such
reasonable rent and for such terms as shall by the inhabitants in vestry be fixed and determined." Section 14
provides that only a shilling rate on the annual value may
be expended in any one year in buying land, erecting
buildings, stocking land, etc., " unless the major part of the
inhabitants and occupiers assessed to the relief of the poor,
in vestry assembled, shall consent thereto, nor until two-
third parts in value of all the inhabitants and occupiers so
assessed (whether present in vestry or not) shall have also
signed their consent thereto in the vestry or parish book."
Section 15 provides for the raising of money which might
be authorised by section 14. Section 16 provides that no
greater " rent " than one shilling in the pound shall be
charged on future rates unless with the consent of two-
third parts in *value* of the proprietors of premises within
the parish. Section 26 refers to Section 7 of the Act of

Elizabeth, and extends the powers of the justices in quarter sessions to the justices in petty sessions. This was to enable the latter to order the father, grandfather, mother, grandmother, or child of the poor, chargeable to the rates, to pay such sum or sums as the justices might think fit.

William IV., 1831, October 15, cap. 42. This Act was to "Amend an Act of the 59th year of George III., for the Relief and Employment of the Poor." Section 1 extends the limit of 20 acres referred to in the 59 George III. to 50 acres, the churchwardens and overseers being empowered "to hire and take on lease" such land "for the employment of the poor," the land to be hired "within or near the parish where the poor are." Section 2 enacts "that it may be lawful for the churchwardens and overseers of any parish to enclose from any waste or common land, or ground lying in or near to such parish, *with the consent in writing of the lord of the manor and the major part in value of the persons having right of common thereupon*, any part or portion of such waste or common land not exceeding 50 acres, and to cultivate and improve the same for the use and benefit of such parish and the poor persons within the same, or to let any part or parts of the same to any poor and industrious inhabitant or inhabitants of such parish, to be by him or them occupied and cultivated on his or their own account." Section 3 extends the provisions hereby given to churchwardens and overseers to "guardians" of those parishes having guardians under the Act 22 George III., cap. 83. Section 4 enacts that all the powers, etc., contained in the 59 George III., cap. 12, with respect to the providing of land for the employment of the poor, or to the cultivation, management, or disposition thereof, etc., "shall, so far as the same are applicable, be deemed and taken to extend to any land provided under this present Act, and to the poor persons employed thereon, or renting any portion thereof respectively."

William IV., 1831, October 20, cap. 59. This Act was to "enable churchwardens and overseers to enclose lands belonging to the Crown for the benefit of poor persons residing in the parish in which such Crown land is situate." After reciting the Act of the 59 George III., section 1 declares "that it shall and may be lawful for the churchwardens and overseers of the poor of any parish to enclose from any forest or waste land belonging to the Crown, lying in or near to such parish, with the consent in writing of the Lord High Treasurer, or the Commissioners of His Majesty's Treasury of the United Kingdom of Great Britain and Ireland for the time being, to be signified by some warrant under his or their hand or hands, any part or portion of such forest or waste lands not exceeding 50 acres, for the purpose of cultivating and improving the same for the use and benefit of such parish and the poor persons within the same."

William IV., 1832, June 1, cap. 42. Section 1, after declaring that "whereas in many parishes enclosed under Acts of Parliament there are in many cases allotments made for the benefit of the poor chiefly with the view to fuel, which are now comparatively useless and unproductive ; and whereas it would tend to the welfare and happiness of the poor if those allotments could be let at a fair rent and in small portions to industrious cottagers of good character, while the distribution of fuel might be augmented by appropriating the said rents to the purchase of an additional quantity," goes on to enact that it "shall and may be lawful" for the trustees of the said allotments, together with the churchwardens and overseers of the poor "in vestry assembled," "and they are hereby required," to let portions of any such allotments "not less than one-fourth of a statute acre and not exceeding one acre, to any one individual according to their discretion, and as a yearly occupation from Michaelmas to Michaelmas (and at such rent as land of the same quality is usually let for in the said parish) to such industrious cottagers of good character, being day labourers or journeymen legally settled in the said parish, and dwelling within or near its bounds, as shall apply for the same in the manner hereinafter mentioned."

Section 8 enacts that the money received from the rents is to be applied "by the vestry in the purchase of fuel, to be distributed in the winter season among the poor parishioners legally settled and resident in or near such parish." Section 10 enacts that "no habitations shall be erected on the portions of land demised under this Act either at the expense of the parish or by the individuals renting the same." Section 11 extends the powers and provisions of the Act to "1 and 2 William IV., cap. 42, and 1 and 2 William IV., cap. 59, in so far as the same may be found applicable." (Already referred to.)

William IV., 1834, August 14, cap. 76. This Act was for "the Amendment and Better Administration of the laws relating to the Poor in England and Wales." Section 21 enacts that except where otherwise provided in the Act, the powers of 22 George III., cap. 83, and 59 George III., cap. 12, and of all other Acts amending them or relating to *workhouses*, the borrowing of money, or relating "in any way to the rural poor," shall "in future be exercised . . . . under the control and subject to the rules, orders, and regulations of the Poor Law Commissioners."

William IV., 1835, September 9, cap. 69. This Act was "to facilitate the conveyance of workhouse or other pro-

perty of parishes, and of Incorporations or Unions of
Parishes in England and Wales." Section 4 provides " that
all the powers and authorities " in the Acts dated 22 George
III., cap. 83 ; 59 George III., cap. 12 ; 1 and 2 William
IV., cap. 42 ; 1 and 2 William IV., cap. 59 ; and 2 and 3
William IV., cap. 42,—" shall in future be exercised (under
the control and subject to the rules, orders, and regulations
of the Poor Law Commissioners) by the overseers of the
poor in any parish not under the management of a Board
of Guardians, and by the guardians of the poor of any union
or parish formed or established by virtue of any statute or
local Act, and all the aforesaid powers relating to the
enclosing, purchasing, hiring, or taking of waste, common,
or other land for the purpose or purposes in the said Acts
mentioned, shall extend and apply to, and may be so
exercised by the said overseers and guardians for the purpose of being used *as a site of a workhouse,* or of being
occupied with a workhouse, or for any other of the purposes of the said recited Act of the 4th and 5th years of
the reign of his present Majesty."

Victoria, 1873, May 15, cap. 19. This Act was for
" Making better provision for the Management in certain
cases of lands allotted under local Acts of enclosure for the
benefit of the Poor." It is generally known as " The Poor
Allotments Management Act, 1873." Section 10 enacts
"that the provision in 2 William IV., cap. 42, whereby
no allotment is to be made of less than one-quarter of an
acre, is hereby repealed." Thus allotments under the Act
of 1873 *may be less* than a quarter of an acre. Section 12
enacts " that notwithstanding anything in the said Act of 2
William IV., cap. 42, it shall be lawful for the authority
executing the powers thereof, or of this Act, to require the
rent for any land let under it to be paid for the whole year

in advance." Section 14 enacts that so much of the said Act of 2 William IV., cap. 42, which provides for the application of rents of land let under the provisions thereof shall not apply to rents for land acquired under any of the Public General Acts passed in the 59th year George III., and the 1 and 2 William IV., cap 59, by guardians and churchwardens and overseers of the poor for the purposes of those Acts, or any of them ; but the rents of such lands shall, after deducting all proper charges, be applied in aid of the poor rate of the parish in which such lands are situate. Section 15 provides that "where any land has been acquired under the said last mentioned Acts, or any of them, for the purposes of those Acts, and such purposes cannot, in the judgment of the Board of Guardians of the parish, or, as the case may be, of the union comprising such parish, be carried into effect, the same lands shall be sold, exchanged, let, or otherwise disposed of in the manner prescribed by the 3rd section of the Act of 5 and 6 William IV., cap. 69." (That section, it may be remarked, gave powers to the overseers and guardians of the poor to sell, purchase, and dispose of workhouse property, and to apply the monies arising therefrom to putting up other buildings, or to such other purpose, for the "permanent advantage" of the parish or union, as might be approved by the Poor Law Commissioners.)

A resumé of the foregoing Acts shows the following result : —Under George III., 1819, cap. 12, sections 12, 13 and 14, it is necessary, before land can be obtained, upon which to employ the "poor," to obtain the "consent of the inhabitants in vestry assembled." It is also necessary, before land can be obtained for "renting" to the "poor," that the same consent should be secured. It is further necessary to obtain the consent of the "major portion of the inhabitants

and occupiers assessed to the relief of the poor," before
more than a 1s. rate can be incurred for purposes of buying
land, erecting the necessary farm buildings, etc. These
obstacles are, we submit, insuperable to even a small number
in any parish obtaining either "employment" (section 12)
or land to "rent" (section 13).   Section 16 puts a further
insuperable difficulty in the way. The Act William IV.,
1831, cap. 42, which professes to extend the powers of the
above Act of George III. (section 12), is still more prohibitory in consequence of the consents which it is first necessary to secure in order to put the Act into force. The Act
William IV., 1831, cap. 59, refers only to "forest" or
"waste" lands belonging to the Crown, and therefore it is
not of general application.

The Act William IV., 1832, cap. 42, refers to what were
and are known as the "fuel" allotments, and cannot by
anyone be considered of particular importance when considering the present day demands in connection with the
general employment on the land of the unemployed by the
local authorities. The Act William IV., 1834, cap. 76,
declares that the powers of the above mentioned Act of
George III., 1819, cap. 12, shall in future be exercised
"under the control and subject to the rules, orders, and
regulations of the Poor Law Commissioners" (now the Local
Government Board). The Act William IV., 1835, cap. 69,
without referring to the last mentioned Act (William IV.,
1834, cap. 76) or to the Act of Elizabeth, declares that all
the powers of the other statutes we name shall, in future, be
exercised (under the control, and subject to the rules, orders,
and regulations of the Poor Law Commissioners) by the
"overseers" in those parishes where there are no Guardians,
and by the *Guardians* in those parishes where there *are*
Guardians. Its directions and provisions are by no means

free from doubt as to the interpretation to be placed upon them. At any rate, the Act does not err in favour of the Labour Leaders in question. The Act of Victoria, 1873, cap. 19, is, again, a further prohibitory one, and makes matters worse for them. It allows the local authorities to claim the rent of allotment or other lands " in advance." In this case, be it remembered, it would be necessary for the *whole year's* rent to be paid in advance, inasmuch as the previous Acts, amended by this of 1873, provide for a *yearly* tenancy from Michaelmas to Michaelmas. In other respects, also, the Act of 1873 limits the scope of previous measures.

It would thus appear that the particular suggestions alluded to at the commencement of this chapter are impossible of adoption. We regret to feel compelled to give such an opinion, but it seems to be the only conclusion one can come to on a careful examination of the Statutes referred to. It must, therefore, be urged that the effort of those who, either not knowing or not properly interpreting the facts of the case, are still requesting the Local Government Board to give their *fiat*, in order to set these ancient statutes in motion, is both wasteful and unfortunate.

It is, however, also argued by some that not only should the unemployed in town and country be put to work under these old statutes; but that municipalities should also take farms on lease, or purchase, and set the unemployed to work upon them. This latter system, it is said, would get rid of much competition between those out of work and those in work, and would not place the stigma of pauperism upon men who would otherwise have to go to the workhouse for Poor Law relief.

Nobody can have greater sympathy than ourselves for those who, willing to work, are unable to obtain it ; but a remedy of

H

the sort here indicated hardly commends itself to us. We agree with the idea that borough authorities, in times of distress, should, if practicable, start works of public utility; but that is a very different thing from asking them to embark in speculative farming for those who are temporarily unemployed. So incongruous is the latter idea, that but for the serious and persistent manner in which it has been put forward, we should view it only with amused amazement.

What are the functions of a municipality? Those functions are such as are connected with public lighting, watching, health, education; but these have nothing to do with municipal distress, which is, in the main, a question either for the charitably-disposed or for the Poor Law to deal with. Those persons elected as members of our large borough councils are usually townsmen. They have little or no practical knowledge of land or farming, and they could not possibly be (nor could they reasonably be expected to be) in constant touch with the lands of the council. Again, it is not possible that artisans—skilled or unskilled— should take to farming work as to the manner born (unless they did so, the whole thing would be a fiasco); and it is absurd to suppose that such men would give constant attendance to the work : they would rightly leave it, directly opportunity offered, for work to which they are accustomed. Above and beyond these considerations there are the interests of the general body of ratepayers to be considered. These ratepayers, forming the bulk of the population, would annually be called upon to meet a large deficit in the interest of a class. Does any one really suppose that they ought to, or would submit to such treatment ? No practical and impartially-minded man will, we venture to assert, give it as his opinion that municipalities in general could "go in" for farming and make it pay, the labour being chiefly, or wholly, obtained from the "unemployed." Unless they could do that, the help afforded to the workers would be mere pauper help, disguise it how we may. Many of the men, too, who would be set to work would be physically unfit for it, and the whole of them would at least be accustomed to other and varied occupations. To expect financial success on a basis such as this is preposterous. Municipalities should adhere to such functions as those we have suggested, and not embark upon work which is neither to the best interests of the workers themselves nor to those of the municipality or of the State. We could wish that some of those responsible persons who advocate municipal farms for the temporary unemployed had a little more acquaintance not merely with what can and cannot be done with land and those whom it is sought to place upon it, but with the just claims also of every section of the community.

By all means let us help men on to the land, but let the men be men who understand the land, and let it be by such means as the Allotments and Small Holdings Acts, and the Local Government Act, 1894. Those Acts, if loyally carried into operation, are destined to revive in England a class of men who at one time were the very backbone of the nation, *viz.*, the old yeomen.

APPENDIX A.

THE Local Government Board has issued the following Orders in connection with the Local Government Act, 1894 :—

(1) AN ORDER AS TO THE COMPULSORY PURCHASE OF LAND, AND AS TO REGULATIONS AND ADAPTATIONS UNDER SECTION 9.

After reciting section 9 (subsections 1-7 and subsections 10, 13) the Order proceeds :—

NOW THEREFORE, We, the Local Government Board, in pursuance of the powers given to Us in that behalf, do, by this Our Order, and until We shall otherwise Direct, Prescribe as follows ; that is to say,—

ARTICLE I.—In every case in which a County Council on a representation by a Parish Council under subsection (2) of section 9 of the Local Government Act, 1894, or on any proceeding under the Allotments Acts, 1887 and 1890, propose to proceed under section 9 of the Local Government Act, 1894, and with a view to such proceeding, to cause public inquiry to be made, the County Council shall, not less than six weeks before the day on which it is proposed that the inquiry shall be held, cause notice to be given in such form and in such manner as are hereinafter prescribed :—(1) The notice shall specify the particulars of the representation, or of the proceeding under the Allotments Acts, 1887 and 1890, and shall state that the County Council propose to cause public inquiry to be made. (2) The notice shall further specify as regards any land proposed to be taken, the quantity and description, and the situation of the land proposed to be taken, the names of the owners, lessees, and occupiers of the said land, and the purpose for which the said land is proposed to be taken. (3) A printed copy of the notice shall be sent by post by the County Council to each owner, lessee, and occupier of the land proposed to be taken, or, if such owner, lessee, or occupier is absent abroad, to his agent.

ARTICLE II.—The County Council, not more than one calendar month, and not less than two weeks before the holding of the public inquiry, shall cause a notice to the like effect as that of the notice prescribed by Article I., and containing also a statement of the day, time, and place appointed for the holding of the inquiry, and of the person or persons by whom the inquiry is to be held, to be published and given in accordance with the following requirements; that is to say,— (1) The notice shall be published in the parish, or, in the case of any proceeding under the Allotments Acts, 1887 and 1890, relating to an urban district, in the district by posting a printed copy of the notice as a bill or placard in every such place in the parish or district, as is ordinarily used for posting public or parochial notices. (2) A printed copy of the notice shall be sent by post by the County Council— (*a*) Where the County Council propose to proceed on a representation of the Parish Council under subsection (2) of section 9 of the Local Government Act, 1894,—to the Parish Council: and (*b*) In the case of any proceeding under the Allotments Acts, 1887 and 1890: (i.) Where the proceeding is taken on a petition under section 2 of the Allotments Act, 1890, by persons qualified as mentioned in that section,—to each of the petitioners. (ii.) Where the proceeding is taken on the petition of the Parish Council,—to the Parish Council. (iii.) Where the proceeding is taken on the petition of the District Council,—to the District Council: and (*c*) In every case to each owner, lessee, and occupier of the land proposed to be taken, or, if such owner, lessee, or occupier is absent abroad, to his agent.

ARTICLE III.—(1) The County Council shall, within ten days after the making of the Order, cause a copy of any Order made by them under section 9 of the Local Government Act, 1894, to be served by post in accordance with the following requirements; that is to say,— (i.) Where the Order relates to land proposed to be taken by the Parish Council for any purpose to which subsection (2) of the said section applies: A copy of the said Order shall be sent by post to the Parish Council. (2) Where the Order relates to land proposed to be taken for the purpose of allotments :—(i.) If the proceeding is taken upon the petition under section 2 of the Allotments Act, 1890, of persons qualified as mentioned in that section, or upon the petition of the Parish Council,—to the Parish Council. (ii.) If the proceeding is taken upon the petition of the District Council,—to the District Council. (3) In every case a copy of the said Order shall be sent by post to each owner, lessee, and occupier of the land proposed to be taken, or, if such owner, lessee, or occupier is absent abroad, to his agent.

ARTICLE IV.—Every copy of a notice or Order which, in pursuance of any provision in Articles I., II., and III., is required to be sent or served by post to or upon any Council or person therein mentioned, shall be so sent or served by a registered letter containing such copy, and properly addressed, prepaid, and posted to such Council or to such person at his usual or last known place of abode.

ARTICLE V.—The period within which a Memorial by a person interested praying that an Order made under section 9 of the Local Government Act, 1894, shall not become law without further inquiry may be presented to the Local Government Board, shall be the period of one calendar month after the making of the said Order.

ARTICLE VI.—For the purposes of section 9 of the Local Government Act, 1894, except so far as by subsection (18), the said section is rendered applicable to a county borough, the several provisions herein-before mentioned of the Allotments Acts, 1887 and 1890, shall be adapted in the form and manner set forth in the schedule to this order.

SCHEDULE.

THE ALLOTMENTS ACT, 1887. Section 2 (2). (2) A County Council or a District Council carrying into effect an Order made under section 9 of the Local Government Act, 1894, for putting in force, as respects land to be taken for the purpose of allotments, the provisions of the Lands Clauses Acts with respect to the purchase and taking of land otherwise than by agreement, shall not under such Order acquire land for allotments save at such price or rent that in the opinion of the said Council all expenses, except such expenses as are incurred in making roads to be used by the public, incurred by the said Council in acquiring the land and otherwise in relation to the allotments may reasonably be expected to be recouped out of the rents obtained in respect thereof.

Section 3 (5), (6), (7) and (8). (5) In construing, for the purposes of section 9 of the Local Government Act, 1894, the provisions of the Lands Clauses Acts as incorporated with the said section, and the provisions of the said Acts, and of sections 77 to 85 of the Railways Clauses Consolidation Act, 1845, as incorporated with an Order which has been made and has become final under the said section, the Local Government Act, 1894, together with any such Order, shall be deemed to be the Special Act ; and the Parish Council, for any purpose for which the said Council are authorised to acquire land by agreement, or for any purpose in relation to which land authorised to be acquired otherwise than by agreement may be assured to the said Council, and the County Council carrying into effect, for such last-mentioned purpose, any such Order as is hereinbefore mentioned, and the County Council or the District Council carrying into effect, for the purpose of allotments, any such Order as is hereinbefore mentioned, shall respectively, as the case requires, be deemed to be the promoters of the undertaking or the company, and the word " land," in relation to any purpose for which the Parish Council are authorised to acquire land, or in relation to allotments, shall have the same meaning as in the Allotments Act, 1887. (6) Where land is purchased under an Order in pursuance of section 9 of the Local Government Act, 1894, otherwise than by agreement, the following provisions shall apply :—(a) The County Council and the Local Government Board shall not make an Order for purchasing any park, garden, pleasure-ground, or other land required for the amenity or convenience of any dwelling-house, or any land the property of a railway or canal company which is or may be required for the purposes of their undertaking : (b) The County Council and the Local Government Board shall, in making an Order for purchasing land, have regard to the extent of land held in the neighbourhood by any owner, and to the convenience of other property belonging to the same owner, and shall, so far as is practicable, avoid taking an undue or inconvenient quantity of land from any one owner. (7) For the purpose of the hiring of land by a Parish Council for a purpose for which the said Council are authorised to acquire land, any person, or body of persons, or body corporate authorised to sell land to the Sanitary Authority for the purposes of the Allotments Act, 1887, may, without prejudice to any other power of leasing, lease land to the Parish Council, without any fine or premium, for a term not exceeding thirty-five years. (8) The County Council and the Local Government Board shall not make an Order in pursuance of section 9 of the Local Government Act, 1894, for purchasing any right to coal or metalliferous ore.

Section 11. (1) Where a Parish Council are of opinion that any land, or any part of any land acquired by the said Council by agreement in pursuance of section 9 of the Local Government Act, 1894, or assured to the said Council in pursuance of subsection (14) of section 9 of the Local Government Act, 1894, for a purpose for which the said Council are authorised to acquire land, is no longer needed for the purpose for which the said land was acquired, or that any other land more suitable for such purpose is available, and may be acquired by the said Council by agreement, the said Council may, with the sanction of the County Council, and subject to the provisions of subsection (2) of section 8 of the Local Government Act, 1894, sell or let such land or part, or exchange the same for other land more suitable for the said purpose, and may pay or receive money for equality of exchange. (2) Where a Parish Council are of opinion that any land, or any part of any land, assured to the said Council in pursuance of subsection (14) of section 9 of the Local Government Act, 1894, for the purpose of allotments, is no longer needed for such purpose, the said Council may, with the sanction of the County Council, and subject to the provisions of subsection (2) of section 8 of the Local Government Act, 1894, sell, or let such land or part, or exchange the same for other land more suitable for the said purpose, and may pay or receive money for equality of exchange. (3) Where a District Council having carried into effect an Order which has been made, and has become final under section 9 of the Local Government Act, 1894, for putting in force for the purpose of allotments the provisions of the Lands Clauses Acts with respect to the purchase and taking of land otherwise than by agreement, are of opinion that any land or any part of any land acquired by the said Council, is no longer needed for the purpose of allotments, or that any other land more suitable for such purpose is available, and may be acquired by agreement, the said Council, with the sanction of the County Council, may sell or let such land or part, or exchange the same for other land more suitable for the said purpose, and may pay or receive money for equality of exchange. (4) The proceeds of a sale under the foregoing provisions of any land, or any part of any land acquired by or assured to a Parish Council, and any money received by the said Council on any such exchange as aforesaid by way of equality of exchange, shall be applied in discharging, either by way of a sinking fund, or otherwise, the debts and liabilities of the said Council in respect of the land acquired or assured as aforesaid, or for any purpose for which capital money may be applied, and which is approved by the Local Government Board ; and the interest thereon (if any), and any money received from the letting of the land may, subject to the provisions of section 8 of the Local Government Act, 1894, be applied in aid of the expenses of the said Council under the Local Government Act, 1894. (5) The proceeds of a sale under the foregoing provisions of any land, or any part of any land acquired by a District Council carrying into effect an Order which has been made and has become final under section 9 of the Local Government Act, 1894, for putting in force for the purpose of allotments the provisions of the Lands Clauses Acts with respect to the purchase and taking of land otherwise than by agreement, shall be applied, and any surplus remaining, any interest, and any money received from the letting of the land, may or shall be applied as nearly as may be in the same manner, and with the same incidents and consequences, as if the said land had been acquired and otherwise dealt with in pursuance of the Allotments Act, 1887. (6) Sections one hundred and twenty-eight to one hundred and thirty-two (both inclusive) of the Lands Clauses Consolidation Act, 1845 (relating to the right of pre-emption of superfluous lands), shall apply upon any sale of any land in pursuance of the foregoing provisions ; but, save as aforesaid, the provisions of the Lands Clauses Consolidation Act, 1845, with respect to the sale of superfluous lands shall not be deemed to be incorporated in section 9 of the Local Government Act, 1894, or in any Order made under that section.

THE ALLOTMENTS ACT, 1890. Section 3. (2) For the purpose of any business under section 9 of the Local Government Act, 1894, relating to any district or parish wholly or partly situate in an electoral division, the County Councillor representing that division shall, if not already appointed, be an additional member of the Standing Committee appointed for the purposes of the Allotments Acts, 1887 and 1890. (3) Any representation by a Parish Council under subsection (2) of section 9 of the Local Government Act, 1894, shall, as of course, and without any Order of the County Council, be referred to the said Standing Committee, who shall forthwith inquire into the circumstances, and shall report the result to the County Council. (4) Where the County Council are satisfied that the circumstances are such as to justify them in proceeding under section 9 of the Local Government Act, 1894, the public inquiry mentioned in subsection (3) of the said section shall be held by such one or more members of the said Standing Committee, or such officer of the County Council as the said Standing Committee may appoint to hold the same.

(2) AN ORDER AS TO THE COMPULSORY HIRING OF LAND FOR ALLOTMENTS : AND AS TO REGULATIONS AND ADAPTATIONS UNDER SECTION 10.

After reciting sections 9 (subsections 1-7, and subsection 13) and 10, the Order proceeds :—

NOW THEREFORE, We, the Local Government Board, in pursuance of the powers given to Us in that behalf, do, by this Our Order, and until We shall otherwise Direct, Prescribe as follows ; that is to say,—

ARTICLE I.—In every case in which a County Council on a representation by a Parish Council under subsection (1) of section 10 of the Local Government Act, 1894, propose to proceed under that enactment, and with a view to such proceeding, to cause public inquiry to be made, the County Council shall, not less than six weeks before the day on which it is proposed that the inquiry shall be held, cause notice to be given in such form and in such manner as are hereinafter prescribed :—(1) The notice shall specify the particulars of the representation, and shall state that the County Council propose to cause public inquiry to be made. (2) The notice shall further specify, as regards any land proposed to be compulsorily hired, the quantity and description and the situation of the land proposed to be compulsorily hired, the period for which it is proposed that the land shall be compulsorily hired, and the names of the owners, lessees, and occupiers of the said land. (3) A printed copy of the notice shall be sent by post by the County Council to each owner, lessee, and occupier of the land proposed to be compulsorily hired, or, if such owner, lessee, or occupier is absent abroad, to his agent.

ARTICLE II.—The County Council, not more than one calendar month and not less than two weeks before the holding of the public inquiry, shall cause a notice to the like effect as that of the notice prescribed by Article I., and containing also a statement of the day, time, and place appointed for the holding of the inquiry, and of the person or persons by whom the inquiry is to be held, to be published and given in accordance with the following requirements ; that is to say,—(1) The notice shall be published in the Parish, by posting a printed copy of the notice as a bill or placard in every such place in the Parish as is ordinarily used for posting public or parochial notices. (2) A printed copy of the notice shall be sent by post by the County Council—To the Parish Council ; and To each owner, lessee, and occupier of the land proposed to be compulsorily hired, or, if such owner, lessee, or occupier is absent abroad, to his agent.

ARTICLE III.—The County Council shall, within ten days after the making of the Order, cause a copy of any Order made by them under section 10 of the Local Government Act, 1894, to be served by post in accordance with the following requirements; that is to say,—A copy of the said Order shall be sent by post to the Parish Council, and to each owner, lessee, and occupier of the land proposed to be compulsorily hired, or, if such owner, lessee, or occupier is absent abroad, to his agent.

ARTICLE IV.—Every copy of a notice or Order which, in pursuance of any provision in Articles I., II., and III., is required to be sent or served by post to or upon any Council or person therein mentioned, shall be so sent or served by a registered letter containing such copy, and properly addressed, prepaid, and posted to such Council, or to such person at his usual or last known place of abode.

ARTICLE V.—The period within which a Memorial by a person interested praying that an Order made under section 10 to the Local Government Act, 1894, shall not become law without further inquiry may be presented to the Local Government Board, shall be the period of one calendar month after the making of the said Order.

ARTICLE VI.—For the purposes of section 10 of the said Local Government Act, 1894, the several provisions hereinbefore mentioned of the Allotments Acts, 1887 and 1890, shall be adapted in the form and manner set forth in the Schedule to this Order.

SCHEDULE.

THE ALLOTMENTS ACTS. Section 2 (2). (2) A Parish Council shall not, under section 10 of the Local Government Act, 1894, or in pursuance of an Order made under the said section, acquire land for allotments, save at such price or rent that, in the opinion of the said Council, all expenses, except such expenses as are incurred in making roads to be used by the public, incurred by the said Council in acquiring the land and otherwise in relation to the allotments, may reasonably be expected to be recouped out of the rents obtained in respect thereof.

Section 3 (5), (6), (7), and (8). (5) In construing for the purposes of section 10 of the Local Government Act, 1894, so far as the said section empowers a Parish Council to hire land by agreement for allotments, and for that purpose provides that section 9 of the Local Government Act, 1894, shall apply as if it were therein re-enacted, with certain modifications, the provisions of the Lands Clauses Acts as incorporated, and of section one hundred and seventy-eight of the Public Health Act, 1875, as applied by subsection (1) of section 9 of the Local Government Act, 1894, the last-mentioned Act shall be deemed to be the Special Act, and the Parish Council shall be deemed to be the Local Authority or the promoters of the Undertaking, as the case requires, and the word "land" shall have the same meaning as in the Allotments Act, 1887. (6) Where land is hired compulsorily by a Parish Council under an Order in pursuance of section 10 of the Local Government Act, 1894, the following provisions shall apply :—
(a) The County Council and the Local Government Board shall not make an Order for the compulsory hiring of any park, garden, pleasure-ground, or other land required for the amenity or convenience of any dwelling-house, or any land the property of a railway or canal company, which is or may be required for the purposes of their undertaking. (b) The County Council and the Local Government Board shall, in making an Order for the compulsory hiring of land, have regard to the extent of land held in the neighbourhood by any owner, and to the convenience of

other property belonging to the same owner, and shall, so far as is practicable, avoid taking an undue or inconvenient quantity of land from any one owner. (7) For the purpose of the hiring of land by a Parish Council for allotments in pursuance of section 10 of the Local Government Act, 1894, any person or body of persons or body corporate authorised to sell land to the Sanitary Authority for the purposes of the Allotments Act, 1887, may, without prejudice to any other power of leasing, lease land to the Parish Council, without any fine or premium, for a term not exceeding thirty-five years. (8) The County Council and the Local Government Board shall not make an Order in pursuance of section 10 of the Local Government Act, 1894, for the compulsory hiring of any right to coal or metalliferous ore.

Section 11. (1) Where a Parish Council are of opinion that any land, or any part of any land, hired by the said Council by agreement, in pursuance of section 10 of the Local Government Act, 1894, for the purpose of allotments, is no longer needed for such purpose, the said Council may, with the sanction of the County Council, and subject to the terms and conditions of the hiring of such land or part, and to the provisions of subsection (2) of section 8 of the Local Government Act, 1894, let such land or part. (2.) Any money received from the letting of the land may, subject to the provisions of section 8 of the Local Government Act, 1894, be applied in aid of the expenses of the Parish Council under the Local Government Act, 1894.

THE ALLOTMENTS ACT, 1890. Section 3 (2), (3), and (4). (2) For the purpose of any business under section 10 of the Local Government Act, 1894, relating to any parish wholly or partly situate in an electoral division, the County Councillor representing that division shall, if not already appointed, be an additional member of the Standing Committee appointed for the purposes of the Allotments Acts, 1887 and 1890. (3) Any representation by a Parish Council under sub-section (1) of section 10 of the Local Government Act, 1894, shall, as of course, and without any Order of the County Council, be referred to the said Standing Committee, who shall forthwith inquire into the circumstances, and shall report the result to the County Council. (4) Where the County Council are satisfied that the circumstances are such as to justify them in proceeding under section 10 of the Local Government Act, 1894, the public inquiry which, by sub-section (3) of section 9 as applied by sub-section (1) of section 10 of the said Act, is required to be made shall be held by such one or more members of the said Standing Committee, or such officer of the County Council as the said Standing Committee may appoint to hold the same.

Note.—The Local Government Board has also issued two other circulars: one being to County Boroughs under section 9 in regard to (a) the compulsory purchase of land, and (b) to certain regulations and adaptations: and the other being to County Councils as to (a) the compulsory hiring of land for allotments, and to (b) certain adaptations of the Lands Clauses Acts. It is unnecessary to reproduce these here.

APPENDIX B.

THE Board of Agriculture has issued the following "Suggested Forms of Rules" under the Small Holdings Act, for the use of County Councils (*see* Section 7) :—

RULES made by the COUNTY COUNCIL of————————————
as to the MODE and CONDITIONS of SALE and LETTING of SMALL HOLDINGS under the SMALL HOLDINGS ACT, 1892.

1. Upon the acquisition of any land required for the purpose of the Act, the County Council shall cause to be set out upon a plan the acreage, situation, and boundaries of each small holding which they propose to sell or let, and the price or rent of the same. Each small holding shall be assigned a distinctive number, and a register of the same shall be kept by the clerk of the County Council. The plan shall be deposited in such convenient place as the County Council may from time to time determine, and shall be open to inspection, free of charge, at all reasonable times by persons applying to inspect the same.

2. Notice of the deposit of the said plan for inspection, and of the fact that the Council are prepared to receive applications for small holdings, shall be given by advertisement in some newspaper circulating in the district, or in such other manner as the County Council may from time to time determine.

3. Applications to purchase or hire a small holding shall be in the form and contain the particulars set out in the Appendix to these Rules. The County Council will print and furnish forms of application free of cost to any person applying for the same.

4. The purchase shall be completed at the expiration of one month after the purchase unless otherwise agreed on.

5. An agreement shall be made between the County Council and an intended tenant, and shall be executed by the Council and such tenant, and shall contain or refer to the particulars set out in the Appendix to these Rules, or be to the like effect.

6. The County Council may from time to time alter any holding which for the time being may be unsold or unlet or the terms thereof, and these Rules shall apply to any holding or terms so altered.

7. These Rules may be executed by a Committee of the County Council constituted under section 16 of the Act.

APPENDIX.

(1.) FORM OF APPLICATION to purchase a SMALL HOLDING.
The Small Holdings Act, 1892.

To the County Council of————————————————————————

I, the undersigned, being willing myself to cultivate the small holding, hereby make application to purchase the small holding numbered —————————————, and situate at——————————————————, in the county of——————————————————, and containing ——————————— acres or thereabouts.

1. Name———————————————————————
2. Residence —————————————————————————
3. Age————————————
4. Occupation ——————————————————————
5.—(1). How much of the purchase money it is proposed to pay down (not less than one-fifth of the whole).
   (2.) How it is proposed to pay the balance.
6. What experience the applicant has had in cultivating land, and what evidence or references can be given as to his being likely to keep the holding in a proper state of cultivation.
   Signature ————————————————— -- _
   Address ——————————————————
   Date ———————————————————

NOTE.—An explanatory Memorandum to the following or the like effect should be endorsed upon or appended as a fly-sheet to the form of application.

Any small holding which may be sold by a County Council must exceed one acre, but is not to exceed 50 acres, or, if it exceeds 50 acres, its annual value, for the purposes of the income-tax, must not exceed 50*l*.

Every small holding sold by a County Council under the Act must, pursuant to the 9th section thereof, for a term of 20 years from the date of the sale, and thereafter so long as any part of the purchase money remains unpaid, be held subject to the following conditions :—

(*a.*) That any periodical payments due in respect of the purchase money shall be duly made.

(*b.*) That the holding shall not be divided, sub-divided, assigned, let, or sub-let without the consent of the County Council.

(*c.*) That the holding shall be cultivated by the owner, and shall not be used for any purpose other than agriculture.

(*d.*) That not more than one dwelling-house shall be erected on the holding.

(*e.*) That any dwelling-house erected on the holding shall comply with such requirements as the County Council may impose for securing healthiness and freedom from over-crowding.

(*f.*) That no dwelling-house or building on the holding shall be used for the sale of intoxicating liquors.

(*g.*) In the case of any holding on which, in the opinion of the County Council, a dwelling-house ought not to be erected, that no dwelling-house shall be erected on the holding without the consent of the County Council.

If any such condition is broken, the Council may, after giving the owner an opportunity of remedying the breach, if it is capable of remedy, cause the holding to be sold.

If on the decease of the owner, while the holding is subject to the conditions imposed by the ninth section of the Act, the holding would, by reason of any devise, bequest, intestacy, or otherwise, become sub-divided, the Council may require the holding to be sold within twelve months after such decease to some one person, and if default is made in so selling the holding, the Council may cause the holding to be sold.

Any such sale by the County Council may be made either subject to the charge in respect of purchase money or free, wholly or partly, from that charge, and in either case the provisions of the Act with respect to the purchase money are to apply in like manner as if the sale were the first sale of a small holding under the Act.

The proceeds of the sale are to be applied in discharge of any unpaid purchase money for the holding, or redemption of any rentcharge or terminable annuity which is not to continue a charge on the holding, and subject as aforesaid are to be paid to the person appearing to the Council to be entitled to receive the same.

The County Council may, under special circumstances, to be recorded in their minutes, sell or consent to the sale under the ninth section of the Act a small holding free from all or any of the conditions imposed by the said section, and may give such consent on such terms as they think fit.

Nothing in or done under the ninth section is to derogate from the effect of any building or sanitary byelaws for the time being in force.

If at any time after the restrictive conditions above mentioned have ceased to attach to a small holding, the owner of the holding desires to use the holding for purposes other than agriculture, he is required before so doing, whether the holding is situate within a town or built upon or not, to offer the holding for sale, first to the County Council, from whom the holding was purchased, next to the person or persons (if any) then entitled to the lands from which the holding was originally severed, and then to the person or persons whose lands immediately adjoin the holding.

By the 20th section of the Act the expressions "agriculture" and "cultivation" include horticulture and the use of land for any purpose of husbandry, inclusive of the keeping or breeding of live stock, poultry, or bees, and the growth of fruit, vegetables, and the like.

(2.) FORM of APPLICATION to Hire a SMALL HOLDING.
The Small Holdings Act, 1892.

To the County Council of————————————————————
I, the undersigned, being willing myself to cultivate the small holding, but unable to buy the same,[1] hereby make application to hire the small holding numbered —————————situate at——————————— in the county of——————————————— and containing——————— acres or thereabouts.

1. Name————————————————————————
2. Residence——————————————————————————
3. Age——————————————————
4. Occupation ——————————————————————
5. What experience the applicant has had in cultivating land, and what evidence or references can be given as to his being likely to keep the holding in a proper state of cultivation.
            Signature——————————————————————
            Address ————————————————————
            Date—————————————————————————

NOTE.—The Board suggests that a copy of the form of agreement into which the applicant will be required to enter in the event of his application being successful should be endorsed upon or appended as a fly-sheet to the form of application.

(3.) PARTICULARS to be contained or referred to in the AGREEMENT to be made between the COUNTY COUNCIL and an intended TENANT.

The holding shall be held subject to the provisions of the Small Holdings Act, 1892, relating to the holdings let by a County Council, and in particular as follows :—

The holding shall not be divided, sub-divided, assigned, let or sublet without the consent of the Council.

The tenant shall himself cultivate the holding, which shall not be used for any purpose other than agriculture, including horticulture, and the use of land for any purpose of husbandry, inclusive of the keeping or breeding of live stock, poultry or bees, and the growth of fruit, vegetables, and the like.

The holding shall be cultivated in a husbandlike manner, according to the custom of the country.

No dwelling-house or building on the holding shall be used for the sale of intoxicating liquors, nor shall any dwelling-house be erected on the holding without the consent of the Council.

If any condition or term of letting is broken, the Council may, after giving the tenant an opportunity of remedying the breach (if it is capable of remedy), determine the tenancy.

The tenant may, before the expiration of his tenancy, remove any

---

[1] If the land has been hired by the County Council, the words "but unable to buy the same" should be omitted.

fruit and other trees and bushes planted or acquired by him for which he has no claim for compensation, and remove any tool-house, shed, greenhouse, fowl-house, or pig-sty, built or acquired by him for which he has no claim for compensation.

If any special provision as to kind or succession of crops, or method of cultivation, or as to repair of buildings be desired, let such be inserted in the agreement. If the land has been hired by the County Council, let there be inserted in the agreement any provisions which may be desirable for the tenant to observe, regard being had to the terms on which the Council hired the land.

A person who will himself cultivate a small holding and is unable to buy it on the terms fixed by the Act, or where the land has been hired by the Council on lease or otherwise, is eligible to become the tenant thereof, and any number of such persons working on a co-operative system, provided such system be approved of by the County Council, are also eligible as tenants of one or more small holdings.

Any small holding which may be let by a County Council must exceed one acre, but is not to exceed 15 acres, or if it exceeds 15 acres its annual value, for the purposes of the income tax, must not exceed 15*l.*

The forms of application numbered 1 and 2 are, of course, not intended to take the place of the formal petition sent in under the Act, of which petition a copy is given in the body of this work (page 67). The two forms referred are for signature by applicants when the County Council is in a position to sell or to let the land to which they refer or are intended to refer.

APPENDIX C.

THE Lord Chancellor has issued the following "Rules" under the Small Holdings Act, 1892 (*see* Section 10):—

1. In these Rules the Small Holdings Act, 1892, is referred to as the Act.

PART I.—REGISTRATION OF LAND ON ACQUISITION BY A COUNTY COUNCIL.—I. *Generally.*—2. Application by a County Council for registration as proprietor, with Absolute Title of land acquired in pursuance of the Act, shall be made in Form 1, or to the like effect, and shall be signed by the Clerk or the Solicitor to, or some other responsible officer of, the Council, and shall be accompanied by a map of the land (prepared according to Rule 6 of the Land Registry Rules, 1889), the conveyance to the Council, and a Statutory Declaration by the Solicitor of the Council, or such other Solicitor as may have been employed by them in the purchase, in Form 2, or to the like effect. 3. If the Council have purchased in consideration of a fee farm or other rent secured by a condition of re-entry or otherwise, whether under section 13 of the Act or under section 10 of the Lands Clauses Consolidation Act, 1845, or if the land is subject to any incumbrance, or if it be known that the mines and minerals are excepted, the fact shall be stated and short particulars given in the Statutory Declaration aforesaid. 4. On receipt of the application the aforesaid Statutory Declaration shall be filed and referred to on the Register, and the Registrar shall register the County Council as proprietors of the land for the purposes of the Act, with an absolute title, if satisfied that they have a good holding title, or, if not so satisfied, he shall register the County Council provisionally pending further investigation, with such other title as is authorised by the Land Transfer Act, 1875; and in the latter case the purchasers from the County Council shall, pending the completion of the absolute registration, have the benefit of the title possessed by the County Council at the time of their provisional registration, and on the registration of such purchasers a note shall be made on the Register accordingly. 5. The completion of the registration with absolute title shall be proceeded with, or may be allowed to stand over for such period and subject to such conditions as the Registrar shall direct. 6. At any time before the actual registration of the title

as absolute any person may lodge a caution against such absolute registration being made, similar to and with the like effect as a caution
against entry of land on the Register. 7. The title of the County
Council may be registered as absolute at such time after the appearance
of the advertisement of the application as the Registrar shall think fit.
8. In the event of any sale of a Small Holding by the County Council,
being either a part or the whole of the land comprised in a title, during
the period between the provisional registration and the completion of
registration, with an absolute title, the County Council shall, nevertheless, proceed to complete the registration with absolute title of the
whole of the land comprised in the provisional registration, and upon
such completion the purchaser of the Small Holding shall be registered
as proprietor with an absolute title of the purchased land. II.—*Investigation of Title under Conveyancing Counsel outside the Office.*—
9. If at any time, either before or after the purchase of land, and either
before or after the leaving of a formal application for registration, the
County Council desire to have the title investigated through the Registry with a view to registration with absolute title, they may apply to
the Registrar for a reference of the title to any land they have purchased, or are about to purchase, to a Conveyancing Counsel, and the
Registrar shall, if he think proper, refer them to such Conveyancing
Counsel (of not less than 10 years standing) as he shall think fit. 10.
The title shall be investigated by such Counsel, and the Conveyance (if
not already settled) shall be settled by him under the instructions of
the County Council, and shall describe the property by reference to the
Ordnance map. 11. If the application for registration by the County
Council is made after the execution of the Conveyance, they shall leave
with the application a report on their title signed by the Conveyancing
Counsel by whom the investigation was made. 12. Such report shall
state whether or not the title of the County Council appears to be a
good holding title, and whether or not there are any qualifications, incumbrances, conditions, exceptions or other matters affecting it, which
ought to be entered on the Register, and, if any, the details thereof.
13. The Registrar may act on such report, and may register the title
as absolute or qualified accordingly, but if it appear to the Registrar
that the title, though open to objection, is one the holding under which
will not be disturbed, he may register the same as absolute or otherwise
proceed under the 17th section of the Land Transfer Act, 1875. 14.
Where the title has already been investigated by any such Conveyancing Counsel as aforesaid, the County Council may request that the
reference be made to such Counsel if the Registrar so think fit. 15.
Where the sale has been completed without the opinion of such Conveyancing Counsel as aforesaid being taken, the title may be referred
and proceeded with in the same manner as above prescribed, as soon as
the application for registration is left in the office.

PART II.—REGISTRATION OF SALES BY COUNTY COUNCIL FOR
SMALL HOLDINGS.—16. On a sale of a Small Holding by the County
Council, the instrument of transfer shall be in Form 3. 17. Where the
whole of the purchase money is not paid on completion, the purchaser

shall execute a charge in Form 4, 5, or 6, with such additions and modification as the circumstances may require. 18. Such charge, so executed, shall be entered on the Register, and shall (subject to the provisions of the Act) operate in all respects as a charge made by a registered proprietor of the land, and may be dealt with on the Register accordingly. 19. An entry shall be made on the Register to the effect that the land was originally acquired under the Act, giving also the date of the sale by the County Council, and showing that the land is subject generally to such of the restrictions and conditions imposed by the Act as may for the time being be subsisting. 20. Such entry may be modified or removed with the consent of the County Council, and on production of a certificate signed by the Clerk or Solicitor, or other responsible officer of the said Council, to the effect that the land is no longer subject to the conditions contained in section 9 of the Act, or that the requirements of section 11 of the Act have been complied with respectively. 21. The cost of the Land Certificate to be issued to the purchaser from the County Council shall, for the purposes of section 6, sub-section (1) of the Act, be included in the costs of registration of title.

PART III.—SALES BY OR WITH THE CONSENT OF THE COUNTY COUNCIL UNDER SECTION 9 OF THE ACT.—22. On any sale made by the County Council under section 9 of the Act, the County Council shall have power to transfer the land, and the instrument of transfer shall be in Form 7 or to the like effect. 23. The provisions hereinbefore contained as to the creation of incumbrances by the first purchaser of a Small Holding shall apply to any such sale. 24. The Transferee shall be registered as proprietor, and suitable entries and cancellations shall be made on the Register according to the terms of the transfer, and no evidence shall be required by the Registrar as to the happening of any of the events mentioned in the said section 9 as giving rise to the powers of the County Council, or the fulfilment of any of the provisions in that section contained.

PART IV.—PROCEEDINGS ON THE DEATH OF THE PROPRIETOR OF A SMALL HOLDING.—25. On the death of the sole proprietor, or of the survivor of several joint registered proprietors of a Small Holding, the Registrar may enter the executor or administrator (if any) as proprietor in the place of the deceased proprietor without regard to the beneficial title. 26. The application for such registration shall be in Form 8. 27. In the exercise of his power as registered proprietor of the land, such executor or administrator shall be a trustee for all persons beneficially interested, and (except for purposes of registered dealings for value with the land) the registration of the executor or administrator shall not affect the beneficial ownership of the land. 28. Production of the probate or letters of administration shall be sufficient proof of the death of the proprietor and of the execution and validity of the will, or the fact of the intestacy. 29. A statutory declaration of identity in Form 9 or to the like effect shall be the only additional evidence required. 30. Where the will is not proved, or no administration is taken out, the Registrar shall proceed as prescribed by section 41 of the Land Transfer Act, 1875.

PART V.—LOCAL OFFICERS.—31. The Registrar may, on the application of the County Council, appoint suitable persons as Local Registrars for the purposes of section 10 of the Act. 32. Every person so appointed shall be either a Barrister or a Solicitor, or an Officer of the County Council, or a District Registrar of the High Court, or a Registrar of the County Court, or a Registrar of an existing Local Deed Registry. 33. The Local Registrar shall supply information to the owners of Small Holdings and other persons in regard to all matters connected with registration and transfer of land under the Act, and shall give all necessary assistance in the preparation of instruments for registration and transfer under the Act. 34. The remuneration of the Local Registrar shall be provided by the County Council, and shall be regulated in such manner as they shall determine. 35. A reasonable contribution to the remuneration of the Local Registrar may, for the purposes of section 6, sub-section (1) of the Act, be included in the cost of registration of title. 36. The persons appointed as hereinbefore mentioned may be removed by the Registrar at any time for incompetence or failure to perform their duties in a satisfactory manner, or (on the application of the County Council) on the ground that the amount of business is insufficient to require such local assistance.

PART VI.—MISCELLANEOUS.—37. Where the land purchased by the County Council is already registered with an indefeasible title under the Land Registry Act, 1862, or with an absolute title under the Land Transfer Act, 1875, the proceedings under these rules shall be modified in such manner as the Registrar may deem convenient. 38. Every instrument of transfer or charge duly executed relating to a Small Holding shall (so far as consistent with the Act) take effect as a conveyance or mortgage by deed, and the provisions of the Conveyancing Act, 1881, shall take effect accordingly, except as varied or negatived in the instrument or by these rules. 39. So long as land is registered as subject to the Act, no transfer (including a transfer by the registered proprietor of a charge) or charge shall be registered without the consent of the County Council, testified by their concurring in the execution thereof. 40. On any sale by the registered proprietor of a charge, the instrument of transfer shall be deemed to have been made in professed exercise of the power of sale (if any) implied in the charge. 41. On any transfer for value of land, made by the registered proprietor of a registered charge or incumbrance conferring a power of sale, it shall be assumed that the transfer is made in exercise of the power, and that the land transferred is sold free from the charge, and from all charges registered subsequently thereto. 42. No purchaser of land, provisionally registered under these rules, or registered with an absolute title, shall (in the absence of express stipulation to the contrary) require any further title beyond that to be obtained by an inspection of the Register, or a certified extract from, or copy of the Register (to be furnished at his expense), and a statutory declaration (at the like expense) as to the existence or otherwise of matters which are declared by section 18 of the Land Transfer Act, 1875, not to be incumbrances within the meaning of that Act. 43. In applying the 3rd and 6th sub-sections of section 83 of the Land Transfer Act of 1875 to Small Holdings, the word "Registrar" shall be substituted for the word "Court." 44. Any land on which a County Council has advanced money under section 19 of the Act may, with the consent of the County Council, be registered, provisionally or otherwise, in like manner and with the like effect as hereinbefore provided with respect to land originally acquired by the County Council for the purposes of the Act. 45. Where land is sold or exchanged by the County Council under section 15 of the Act, the instrument of transfer shall contain additions in Form 10 or to the like effect. 46. On receipt of such transfer, the Registrar shall register the Transferee without further enquiry as to the fulfilment of the provisions of the said section, and shall cancel all references to the Act that may have been entered on the Register and that no longer affect the land. 47. Except as varied by these rules, the existing rules made under the Land Transfer Act, 1875, shall apply to Small Holdings. 48. These Rules may be cited as The Land Registry (Small Holdings) Rules, 1892, and shall commence on the 1st October, 1892.

SCHEDULE OF FORMS UNDER THE FOREGOING RULES.

FORM 1.

APPLICATION BY A COUNTY COUNCIL FOR FIRST REGISTRATION AS PROPRIETORS OF LANDS.

Land Registry.

LAND TRANSFER ACT, 1875, AND SMALL HOLDINGS ACT, 1892.

No. of Title————————

The County Council of ——————————————————————
apply to be registered as proprietors with Absolute Title of the land shewn and edged with red on the accompanying map marked ———————————————, which land is also comprised in the accompanying Conveyance marked —— ——————————————— and is also referred to in the accompanying statutory declaration marked——————————————.

   Dated the—————of————————189—.

[Signature of the Clerk, Solicitor, etc., to the Council.]

The address for service of the said Council is at ——————————————

FORM 2.

STATUTORY DECLARATION TO ACCOMPANY APPLICATION IN FORM

Land Registry.

LAND TRANSFER ACT, 1875, AND SMALL HOLDINGS ACT, 1892.

No. of Title————————

In the matter of the application of the County Council of————

—————————————————

   I,——————————————————————
of——————————————————————
Solicitor, do solemnly and sincerely declare as follows :—

   I acted for the above-named Council in the purchase of the land shewn and edged with red on the map marked————————now produced and shewn to me.   As such Solicitor I examined the

135

Vendor's title in manner following [here state particulars of examination, length of title shewn, name of Counsel (if any) employed, special conditions (if any), comparison of abstract, name and address of Vendor and Vendor's Solicitor, etc., etc.].

The investigation so made was, in my opinion, as full an investigation of the Vendor's title as was reasonably possible and suitable under the circumstances of the case.

I (or the said Counsel where employed) advised that the title was a good holder's title, and I know of nothing which would lead me to suppose that there is any adverse claim in existence against it.

The said land has been duly conveyed to the said Council (subject to the incumbrances, leases, conditions, the farm rent, etc., etc., set forth in the Schedule hereto).

From the above consideration I am able to state that the said Council have a good holding title to the said land (subject as aforesaid).

THE SCHEDULE.

And I make, etc.

FORM 3.

INSTRUMENT OF TRANSFER ON A SALE OF A SMALL HOLDING BY THE COUNTY COUNCIL.

Land Registry.

LAND TRANSFER ACT, 1875, AND SMALL HOLDINGS ACT, 1892.

No. of Title ————

of ———— 189—. In consideration of £————[and *if so* of the perpetual rent charge of £ —— — secured by instrument of even date herewith, *or otherwise as provided by section 6 of the Act*], the County Council of———————————hereby transfer to ————————————————————————

of —————————————————————————

all the land [shewn and edged with red on the map marked —————————— sealed by the said Council and also signed by or on behalf of the said Transferee being part of the land] comprised in the title above referred to for the purposes of a Small Holding under the Small Holdings Act, 1892.

The
Seal of the
County
Council.

FORM 4.

PERPETUAL RENT CHARGE TO SECURE PART OF PURCHASE MONEY
FOR A SMALL HOLDING.

Land Registry.

LAND TRANSFER ACT, 1875, AND SMALL HOLDINGS ACT, 1892.

No. of Title ————

———————————— *of* ———————————*189*—. To secure £—————————, part of the purchase money of the land [shewn and edged with red on the map marked ———————————, signed by me, being part of the land] comprised in the title above referred to I,————————————————————————

———————————————————————————

of—————————————————————————

———————————————————————————

hereby charge the said land with the payment to the County Council of—————————————————————————
of a perpetual yearly rent charge of £ —————— ——————
payable on the ————————————of———————— —.—
the ——————————— of————————————— in every year.

The charge will be printed on a double folio, similarly to charges . made under the Land Registry Rules of 1889, to be obtained at the Registry.

N.B.—Sec. 44 of Conveyancing Act, 1881, combined with Rule 38, gives necessary powers of distress and entry.

FORM 5.

CHARGE REPAYABLE BY HALF-YEARLY INSTALMENTS TO SECURE PART OF PURCHASE MONEY FOR A SMALL HOLDING.

Land Registry.

LAND TRANSFER ACT, 1875, AND SMALL HOLDINGS ACT, 1892.

No. of Title————————

of——————————————— 189—. To secure £—————, part of the purchase money of the land [shewn and edged with red on the map marked———————, signed by me, being part of the land] comprised in the title above referred to, I ———————————

———————————————————————————

of—————————————————————————
hereby charge the said land with the payment to the County Council of————————————————of the sum of £ —————— payable by the————————————half-yearly instalment of £————— with interest at ——————— per cent. per annum on the amount for the time being remaining unpaid on the—————of————— and the—————of——————— in every year.

The charge will be printed on a double folio, similarly to charges under the Land Registry Rules of 1889, to be obtained at the Registry.

N.B.—All further necessary powers are in Secs. 22 to 28 of the Land Transfer Act and Conveyancing Act, 1881, Secs. 19 to 22 and Rules 38 and 40.

FORM 6.

TERMINABLE ANNUITY TO SECURE PART OF PURCHASE MONEY FOR A SMALL HOLDING.

Land Registry.

LAND TRANSFER ACT, 1875, AND SMALL HOLDINGS ACT, 1892.

No. of Title —————— .

of —————————— 189—. To secure £————, part of the purchase money of the land [shewn and edged with red on the map marked————————, signed by me, being part of the land] comprised in the title above referred to, and interest thereon at ———— per cent. per annum, I ——————

—————————————— of ——————————

hereby charge the said land with the payment to the County Council of—————————of an Annuity of £————for———— years payable half-yearly on the ————day of ———— and the————of:——————————in every year.

The charge will be printed on a double folio, similar to charges under the Land Registry Rules of 1889, to be obtained at the Registry.

N.B.—Sec. 44 of Conveyancing Act, 1881, combined with Rule 38, gives necessary powers of distress and entry.

FORM 7.

INSTRUMENT OF TRANSFER ON SALE BY COUNTY COUNCIL UNDER SECTION 9 OF THE SMALL HOLDINGS ACT, 1892.

Land Registry.

LAND TRANSFER ACT, 1875, AND SMALL HOLDINGS ACT, 1892.

No. of Title————

of ————189—. In consideration of £————[and *if so* of the perpetual rent-charge of £————secured by instrument of even date herewith, *or otherwise as provided by section 6 of the Act*], and by virtue and in pursuance of section 9 of the Small Holdings Act, 1892, the County Council of ————————— ——————————————hereby transfer to———————— ——————————of————————

———————————————————————the land comprised in the title
above referred to [free from the charge (*s*)] dated the————————of
————————18——, and the ——————of————————18——,
and the annuity dated the————————————————of————————18——,
registered against the said title [as the case may be], and free
from the conditions (*b*), (*c*), (*d*), etc., of sub-section I of the said
section 9 of the said Act.

Seal of the
Council,

FORM 8.

APPLICATION FOR REGISTRATION OF THE EXECUTOR OR
ADMINISTRATOR OF A DECEASED PROPRIETOR.

Land Registry.

LAND TRANSFER ACT, 1875, AND SMALL HOLDINGS ACT, 1892.

No. of Title ————————

A. B., of————————————————————————————————————

the Executor [Administrator] of C.D., of ————————————————
deceased, the registered proprietor of the above title, hereby applies
for registration in his place.

Dated the————————————————of———————————— 189—.

[Signature of Executor (or Administrator)
or his Solicitor.]

FORM 9.

STATUTORY DECLARATION OF IDENTITY OF A TESTATOR
OR INTESTATE.

Land Registry.

LAND TRANSFER ACT, 1875, AND SMALL HOLDINGS ACT, 1892.

No. of Title ————————

I——of
————————————————————————————————— solemnly and sincerely
declare as follows :—

I knew C. D. ——————————————— of——————————————————————————————————— the Testator [Intestate] named in the Probate [Letters of Administration] now produced and shewn to me marked ————————————— . The said C. D. was, to the best of my knowledge and belief, the same person as the C. D. of———[Registered address] named in the Register under the title above referred to——————

And I make, &c.——————————————————————————————

FORM 10.

ADDITIONS TO INSTRUMENT OF TRANSFER ON SALE UNDER SECTION 15 OF "THE SMALL HOLDINGS ACT."

(1.) After " In consideration of £———————————" add " and by " virtue and in pursuance of Section 15 of The Small Holdings Act, " 1892."

(2.) At the end of the Instrument add " to hold the same free " from all obligations and liabilities under or by reason of the said " Act."

APPENDIX D.

TYPES OF ENGLISH PEASANTRY.

I.

The above is a portrait of the small-holder (Mr. B——) referred to on page 90.

TYPES OF ENGLISH PEASANTRY.

II.

TYPES OF ENGLISH PEASANTRY.

III.